LATIGO'S CHOICE

ALSO BY PATRICK LINDSAY

Opening the Frontier: Spencer and Son

LATIGO'S CHOICE

TAMING THE WEST

LATIGO BOOK ONE

PATRICK LINDSAY

WOLFPACK
PUBLISHING
— EST 2013 —

Latigo's Choice: Taming the West
Paperback Edition
Copyright © 2024 (As Revised) Patrick Lindsay

Wolfpack Publishing
1707 E. Diana Street
Tampa, FL 33610

wolfpackpublishing.com

Paperback ISBN 978-1-63977-619-1
eBook ISBN 978-1-63977-663-4

LATIGO'S CHOICE

PROLOGUE

COLORADO, 1838

B arnabus Smith knew he was in trouble. He thought he and his buddy Ezekiel Dunne had gotten the easy job. Their fellow fur trappers had more pelts than they could carry around back in the Rocky Mountains. Somebody had to take the furs to Los Angeles and exchange them for money. The rest of them would follow when they had worked the rich western slopes of the Rockies just a little longer.

Things had started out fine. Barnabus and Zeke had left three days ago with just their horses plus two pack horses, carrying the furs and things they would need on the trail to Los Angeles. They'd been talking from the minute they left camp about what they would do when they reached Los Angeles with the money they would have in their pockets.

That was before the Ute war party had picked up their trail about fifty miles back.

Barnabus was just glad some young buck had let out a war cry as they started closing in. They'd been too busy talking about Los Angeles instead of checking their back trail. Tenderfoot mistake. It had almost been a silent slaughter. That one war cry gave them a chance to skedaddle.

They still had a chance to get away, only because of pure luck. They'd been climbing a mesa—one of many on the Colorado Plateau. Barnabus had needed to get himself a look from the top so he could map out their trail for the next hundred miles or so. That's why they were pointed toward this mesa. Now, even with the packhorses in tow, they stood a good chance to reach the top and command the high ground.

Barnabus put his boots to his horse, then cut the pack horse loose as they neared the top. He didn't look to see if Zeke did the same. There wasn't time. Barnabus vaulted out of the saddle as they reached the top. He looked below and saw that the Utes were strung out, climbing the mesa and letting the war cries loose as they came.

Barnabus grabbed his Hawken rifle from the saddle, thankful he had loaded it and double-checked this morning. He knew Zeke had done the same. He checked his waistband. His brand-new five-shot Paterson Colt was there. It had cost him an arm and a leg in St. Louis this spring, but it might just be the thing that allowed him to keep his hair.

Barnabus steadied the Hawken on a rocky ledge, took aim, and touched 'er off, emptying the saddle of the Ute riding out front. Zeke's rifle boomed on his left, and a second pony was running free.

A warrior came over the top, leaning low against the pony's flank and swinging a tomahawk. The war cries up close were enough to curdle a man's blood. Barnabus drew the Paterson Colt and cut him down. He could hear Zeke's pistol shot on his left. He knew that was the only pistol shot Zeke had.

Barnabus risked a shot at the Ute closing in on Zeke's position. It wasn't a clean hit, but he saw the warrior spin around. Looking to his front, he saw nothing for a few seconds, then a warrior rose from the ground and dove at him. Barnabus raised the Colt enough to fire a shot directly into the Ute's belly.

Shoving the dying brave away from him, Barnabus struggled to his feet and looked around. There were two warriors retreating down the hill. Looking to his left, Barnabus saw Zeke locked in a hand-to-hand battle with the last brave, fighting off thrusts from the Ute's knife.

Barnabus rushed across the mesa and fired a shot into the warrior's head. The Ute tumbled away, and Zeke collapsed to the ground, bleeding from cuts to his cheek and his arm.

Barnabus kneeled beside his partner. "You okay?" he puffed, peering at the wounds.

Zeke struggled to sit up. "Yeah, he jest scratched me," he answered. He struggled to get his breath, looking around. "They all gone?" he asked.

Barnabus took another look down the hill and nodded. "All gone," he confirmed. Zeke's cuts were a lot more than scratches, but they could patch him up.

Zeke pushed himself to his feet and nodded at the Paterson Colt in Barnabus's right hand. "Remind me to get me one of them when we git to Los Angeles," he said.

They rested on the mesa top for a few hours after rounding up the packhorses and bandaging Zeke's knife wounds. Zeke took a few minutes to rest while Barnabus got his bearing from the mesa top and explored a little.

Zeke looked around a little later to see Barnabus returning to the horses with a hatful of what looked like black rocks. He took them from his hat, one by one, and put them into his saddlebag.

"What're you doin', weightin' down your hoss with rocks like that?" Zeke demanded.

Barnabus finished emptying his hat and turned around to make a return trip to where he'd found the rocks. He shrugged. "I've got a hunch they might be copper," he said. "Worth a few bucks in Los Angeles." He looked over and pointed at Zeke's horse. "I wanna put a few in yore saddlebag, too," he informed Zeke.

Zeke rolled his eyes. "You're plumb crazy," he flared. "I ain't puttin' no extry weigh on my hoss all the way to Californy."

Barnabus looked injured. "Did I jest save yore hide or what?" he asked.

Zeke stared at the ground and moaned. "Okay, but no more'n a few pounds," he said. "An' know this, it's the first thing I chuck outta the saddlebags if my hoss starts to gettin' tuckered out."

The trip to Los Angeles took another ten days. Barnabus and Zeke quit talking and took to watching the back trail for the rest of the way, but there were no more war parties. They decided on doing first things first when they trotted into town. The first stop took them to a trading post, where they bargained for a good price on the furs. The second and third stops were both saloons.

It wasn't until about noon on the second day in town that Barnabus decided to do something about the black rocks. He asked around and got directed to a trader who could check the rocks and tell him what he had. Folks at the boarding house said he was honest. Barnabus had no choice but to trust him—they just looked like black rocks. Barnabus was betting on his hunch.

Zeke waited on a bench outside while Barnabus carried both saddlebags inside. The midday sun had Zeke sweating pretty hard and thoroughly irritated by the time Barnabus came out and put the saddlebags back on the horses.

Barnabus sat down on the bench and said nothing, just staring at the ground. Zeke was out of patience.

"Well, what'd he say?" Zeke demanded.

Barnabus reached into this pocket, took out three hundred dollars and gave it to Zeke, whose eyes rounded to the size of silver dollars. He counted twice, then started over.

"Three hunnerd," Barnabus informed him, saving

Zeke the trouble of counting two or three more times. "It was gold. Them black rocks was gold."

Zeke's mouth opened and closed a few times without saying anything. "Gold?" he finally squeaked.

"Yup." Barnabus shifted on the bench and said nothing else.

"If'n it were gold, how come it was all black like that?" Zeke demanded.

Barnabus shrugged. "He said it was oxi-sumthin'."

"Oxi-sumthin'?" Zeke said, his voice getting higher as he talked. "Oxi-sumthin'? What's oxi-sumthin'?"

Barnabus shrugged again. "Don't rightly know," he admitted. "The rocks got plumb black, jest a-settin' out in the sun like that, but they was gold, all the time."

Zeke was out of questions. He shoved the money into his pocket and they both sat in silence on the bench for several minutes.

"We've got to remember where that mesa was," Barnabus said after a while. "There was three of 'em lined up, and this was the tallest one, right in the middle. Mebbe that can help us find it again."

"Yeah," Zeke said without enthusiasm. "The one in the middle." He cleared his throat and stared at his boots. "Of course," he reminded Barnabus, "we'd hafta go back out there where that Ute war party jumped us. It were right in the middle of that."

Barnabus winced and nodded. "Right," he agreed. "In the middle of all them Utes."

Zeke waited a couple minutes before speaking. "Of course, we don't have to go right now, do we? I still got to get me one of them Paterson Colts."

Barnabus stared down the street. There were several saloons they hadn't tried yet. "Not right away," he agreed. "Maybe we can go back in a few days. Or a week or two."

ONE
MESSAGE FROM THE PAST

FREDERICKSBURG, TEXAS, 1879

This guy had been wantin' to have it out with me for a few weeks now. He'd finally pushed me one step too far, so there we were, having a knuckle-and-skull fight in the middle of Main Street. And this was my last day as deputy sheriff in this county, of all things.

The sheriff, Pike Hardy, was sittin' comfortably on a bench outside the general store. I guess he figured I could take care of this, which I could. The new deputy, who'd been deputy before me, went by the name of Boone. Boone had collected some bets and was just standing off to the side a little, making sure it was a fair fight.

This guy, who went by the name of Lunk, had slept it off in my jail last night. He was sober now, but he'd spent too many nights in the saloon sucking down the suds to be in shape. His tongue was just about hangin' out, and his right eye was all swole up where I'd connected with my left hand a few times. We'd been throwing punches for about five minutes now, and he already looked pretty tuckered out.

I could tell he wanted to rush me and get me down on the ground. He gathered himself and charged me, but I could see him coming all the way. I took one step sideways and stuck my foot out. He went down in a heap and roosted there on the street for a minute.

Lunk gathered himself up with a roar and came straight in at me, his right fist cocked back there around his ear. He had his dander up after that tripping. He got about a foot away from me and started to swing that big right fist. I stepped in and lifted my left fist to his chin. He fell to his knees, then went straight down on his face. I could hear the air whoosh right out of him.

I stepped back, rubbin' my knuckles and thinking this was a tough start for the day. I'd been deputy sheriff for about a year to Pike Hardy, and some days were harder than others. Today was my last day, though. I'd go out with sore knuckles, I could tell.

My name is Latigo Smith, although most folks call me Lat. I'm about six feet one and one hundred ninety pounds, so most folks don't want to tangle with me like this. Lunk wasn't the smartest guy in town, and he'd just proved it again. I prodded him with my foot.

"Come on, Lunk," I told him. "Let's get you down to the doc's office."

"I kin go myself," he mumbled, hoisting himself up off the street. He steered himself toward the doctor's office. "Nice punch," he added, staggering away.

I looked around. Boone was counting money, chuckling. "I'll buy you a beer," he offered.

I looked over at Pike Hardy. "Good job, keeping that left hand down, like I told you," he said. "It set him up nice for that last punch."

I grinned and followed after Boone, rubbing my face as I went. Lunk had gotten in one good shot. I wondered if it would bruise. Not that it mattered that much. I was leaving town, and I'd be on the trail for a while. I wasn't sure if a bruise would look that bad. I didn't worry about that a lot. A couple of the ladies have said I'm handsome, but they didn't look real sure of themselves when they said it.

I joined Boone in the saloon for a quick beer, then headed out to work my last day. Tonight, I would have dinner with Pike and his wife, Norah. Boone and his wife would probably join us. Then I would be off to Colorado, heading home after almost two years in Texas.

━━━

I stared out the window of my room at the boarding house. I had been in Fredericksburg a year now, and I'd been in Texas or New Mexico for more than another six months before that. It was early in June, but the heat of the day still clung to my skin. Texas had been good to me, but it wasn't home. I guess that's why I had chosen an uncertain future back in Colorado. I had stewed over this decision long enough, then finally made my choice.

The Hardys had built themselves a ranch house on

some property east of town. I mounted up and moved in that direction. I had everything I was going to take with me, but it wasn't much. My horse could carry it all. I would stay the night with the Hardys, then ride out to Austin to take the train home.

I grinned to myself as I urged the horse to a trot, leaving Fredericksburg behind me for good. My plan had been to ride out to Colorado, but the Hardys, and even Boone, had convinced me to take the train. Other than a fast trip up to Ft. Worth one time, the train ride would be a new thing for me. At twenty-six, I was too young to turn down new things.

I reached the Hardy's place before Boone and his wife. Pike met me at the door and took me inside to say hello to Norah. She gave me a hug and reminded me she had planned to find me a girl. Now, she told me, that would be somebody else's job.

Pike handed me a whiskey, and we settled down on the front porch. Boone arrived with his wife, Alice, and joined us on the porch. Pike swirled the whiskey around in his glass and looked at me.

"Lat," he said, "we're sorry to see you go. We understand about goin' home, and finding new adventure and all. Norah and me wish you the best. You're a good man. This town and this county are a safer place, and…well, we're grateful to you."

Boone shifted around in his chair and waved his hand in the air. "Don't go gettin' all mushy over there, Pike," he said. "You done good here, Lat," he said. "That's what he's trying to say. Plus, I made some good money bettin' on your fight today."

I knew that was high praise from Boone. We talked

a little about Colorado, and I asked them what they knew about the railroads being built up there and how that might change things. Before I knew it, the ladies had called us in for dinner.

After the meal, we settled down in the living room, and Pike asked me if I had any relatives that I knew of back in Denver or somewhere.

I shrugged. "I've lost track of any family a long time ago," I said. "My ma died when I was maybe ten, and my dad before I was twenty. My dad had one brother, older than him, who was a mountain man, livin' in the high country, that's what Pa said. I never met him."

Pike stared over at Norah, then looked back at me. "Did your pa tell you his name?" he asked.

"Barnabus," I said. "Barnabus Smith."

Pike and Norah looked at each other for a minute, then Pike got up and left the room. I heard him rummaging around in another room, then he came back with an old, yellowed piece of paper, which he gave to me.

"You know," he told me. "I was raised by an old mountain man named Jed Hardy, not too far from here. He was from Colorado, though, and I think he only stayed here to raise me. After I was grown, he went back."

He stared down at his hands and looked over at Norah, who nodded at him. "Thing is," Pike said, "I found an old box in the shack where I grew up, things that belonged to Jed Hardy, and some papers for me. This old letter was in there, too, but I never knew what to do with it until now."

I took the paper and opened it, afraid it would fall apart on me—it was that old and crumbly. My eyes dropped to the name at the bottom. The writing was pretty cramped and messy, but that name at the bottom jumped out: Barnabus Smith.

I stared across the room at the Hardys. I'd never mentioned my uncle's name, and there are so many Smiths around, I knew they hadn't ever thought it might be my uncle. I looked back down at the letter.

"Go ahead and read it out loud if you want to," Pike said.

I spread it out on my knee. Norah brought a candle over and put it on the table next to me. It took me a minute to get the hang of the funny looping letters and the way Barnabus wrote them, but then I started to read:

Dear Jed,

I know you is plannin' to raise that young 'un down there. Hope it's goin' well for ya. I'm out in Californy and I bin back to Colorado a time or two. I don't expect to be back an' I ain't seen old Ezekiel Dunne in some years neither. That's why I'm writin' you, just in case you ever go back.

Zeke and I was haulin' pelts to Los Angeles back in 1837 or somethin' like that—cain't exackly remember. It were a couple year after we done the fur trappin' on the western slopes. Anyhow, Zeke and me got attacked by a

war party of them Utes on the way. We clumb
up a mesa an' stood 'em off OK. Zeke taken a
shot in the shoulder, but it warn't to bad. We
made it to Californy with the pelts and our
scalps. The thing is, I scouted around that
mesa top whilst Zeke was pullin' hisself
together. I found some black rocks an' I taken
'em to Los Angeles cause I thought they was
copper. Turned out to be gold. I ain't kiddin'.
Zeke said he'd seen some little'uns before but I
don't know. Never got back for anuther 20
years. Never mind why. I bin back twice since
then, lookin' for that mesa. Never found it
again. Not doin' too good now, so I figgered I'd
tell you, in case you ever git out that way.

We wuz runnin' on a line from Ouray,
going south and west to Durango, then Los
Angeles. Mebbe a hunnerd miles outta
Durango.

Good luck to ya.

-Barnabus Smith

I looked up from the letter. Pike was watching me.
I didn't know what to think.

"Gold?" I asked. "I mean, I know they've found a
lot of gold out there. Pike's Peak and all that. But I've
never heard of gold in black rocks. Have you?"

Pike shook his head, and I looked over at Boone. I

knew right away that was a mistake. He was gathering himself up for a story, I could tell.

"I ain't never heard of gold comin' from black rocks, but I've heard tell of some interestin' gold stories, let me tell you," Boone started out. He reached into his pocket for a cigar, but one look from his wife Alice froze him in his tracks.

"Well, anyway," Boone went on. "This here story is about a Dutch guy, name of Jacob something-or-other. Found him some gold in the Suspicion Mountains, out there in Arizona."

"Superstition Mountains," Alice told him.

"Huh?" Boone was totally thrown off.

"Superstition Mountains."

"Right. Anyhow," Boone continued, this Dutchie found hisself some gold, way back in them mountains. Dutchie turned out to be pretty smart—he never took out too much gold all at once, an' he never told nobody else where it was."

Boone leaned back and made himself comfortable. I'd never seen him happier than when he had a crowd to listen to one of his yarns.

"Word got out, and lots of folks come lookin' for that gold," he continued. "They come through the desert in all that heat, then went into the mountains. Some of 'em froze up there. Some others got kilt by the Apaches. There was somebody else, Doctor Thorn, said he got caught by Injuns and they showed him a bunch of gold up there. They set him loose an' he got a bunch of folks to go back with him to look for the gold. Never found it. Buncha those folks died, too."

He looked around to make sure everybody was

still listening. "Nobody never found that gold," he said. "Dutchie died and nobody knows where it is."

Boone sat up, pleased with his story, and reached for his shirt pocket again. He looked over at Alice and dropped his hand back into his lap. He looked over at me.

"I'm just sayin'," he said.

"Saying what?" I asked. "Are you saying I'm gonna die if I go looking for those black rocks?"

Boone shrugged.

"I won't be looking anyway," I said. "A mesa top somewhere between Silverton and Los Angeles could be anywhere." I looked over at Pike Hardy. "Thanks for the letter, Pike," I said. "That must have been my Uncle Barnabus, like you thought. He was the only family I knew of after my folks died."

We moved back into the dining room for some dessert and coffee, then we talked late into the night. When I finally went to sleep in a guest room at the Hardy's place, I knew it would be my last night in Texas for a long time. Maybe I would never be back. By tomorrow, I would be catching a train in Austin.

Still, I thought as I drifted off to sleep, gold was a thing to think about. Like lots of folks from Colorado, I'd done my share of thinking about making a gold strike. Not from black rocks, though. I'd never heard of that.

▭

Leadville was what you would call a boom town. I hadn't seen anything like it, really, but I wasn't there when Pike's Peak went crazy several years ago. I got off the train and stretched, feeling downright cramped after the days I'd spent bouncin' down the tracks. At least I was here now. I went down to fetch my horse when they unloaded him.

A livery stable was the first thing I looked for. I found one fast enough, but my eyebrows went up when the old gent told me how much it would cost. I figured it was maybe the same all over town, though. I knew they could charge a lot when there was money from gold and silver flowing into the town. I paid and moved on down the main street.

Leadville hadn't even been a place on the map when I'd left a few years ago. Folks had been mining at a place called California Gulch, just a piece down the road from here. They hadn't found much gold like they were hopin' for, and they got just plain irritated when some heavy sludge kept blocking up their sluice boxes. What they eventually found was that the heavy black stuff in the sluice boxes was high-grade silver.

Now Leadville was a big town. People had moved out of a bunch of tents and made themselves a town with banks, hospitals, cafés, churches, and a big school. And saloons. Lots of saloons. I strolled down the street. I could hear a little blasting powder goin' off not too far away. I could hear axes and hammers from all the building. Now and then, I could hear a gunshot. Having just got here from Texas, I was kinda used to that.

I knew the kind of hard work it took to bring gold or silver out of those mountains and streams. That part didn't scare me. The thing is, it looked to me like I needed to be here a couple of years ago, back before everybody and his brother were out there staking claims and working the land.

There were lots of crooks in town, too. Card sharps, pickpockets, robbers, you name it. Having been a deputy, I knew 'em when I saw 'em. A man would have to work to keep his money if he found it. Maybe that was the best way to make money around here, helping others protect what they had.

Or maybe, I thought, I needed to check into working for the railroads. It had been a long trip to get here, but it was a lot faster than I could have made it on horseback, and I didn't have to watch out for highwaymen and war parties. I could picture how railroads could really put this country together.

All this thinking was making me thirsty. I walked along for a few more blocks. I made a note of a boarding house that looked like it might work for me, then I stopped in front of a saloon. I stared at the sign overhead. It said: *Whiskey Wagon.* I grinned and went inside.

I saw miners just about everywhere I looked. There were a lot of glasses clinking and a lot of belly-laughing going on. The air was thick with tobacco smoke and the smell of whiskey. Just what I'd expected.

I looked around for the bar. There was a long, heavy board running down the side of the room, and behind that was a bartender with a mustache that went on for days. I stepped up and ordered a whiskey, tossed it down, and decided it was drinkable. I ordered another from Mustache Man and went looking for a seat.

"You kin sit here if you want."

I looked around and saw a guy probably about my age, maybe six inches shorter but built like a bull. Blond hair and a friendly face. I didn't really see any other empty seats, so I took him up on his offer.

"Latigo Smith," I said and stuck out my hand.

A serving girl at the table next to us whirled around and stared at me. I'd never seen her before. "Ma'am," I said, taking off my hat and putting it on the table. She didn't answer, just quit staring and hurried off.

"Holt Burns," the blond guy said, shaking my hand. He had him a powerful grip, I'll give him that. He stared at the serving girl who'd just hurried away. "You know her?" he asked.

I shook my head. "Never saw her before," I told him.

"Huh," said Holt Burns, staring after her. "I think mebbe she knows you."

TWO

TRUSTING STRANGERS

I stared at the serving girl and shook my head. "I'm sure I never saw her," I said. "Besides, I just got into town a couple hours ago."

"Huh," said Holt. "It was when you said your name that she really jumped." He stopped to down his beer and shrugged. "Anyway," he said, "you just got into town? What do you plan to do around these parts?"

I waved for a beer, wondering if that same serving girl would bring it over. "Don't know yet," I said to answer his question. "I was thinking maybe some mining work when I got here, but I think maybe there's too many folks doing that already."

I stopped when the same serving girl brought my beer. She didn't really look at me this time, just kinda glanced at me sideways and hurried away. I got to admit, I thought she was pretty. Blond hair and blue eyes. Maybe a couple years younger than me.

I looked back over at Holt and he was grinnin' at

me. "She didn't look like she paid you no attention this time," he said.

"Yeah, that sounds like my story," I told him. "What's your story? Where you from? Doesn't sound like you're from around here."

"Nope, not from around here," he agreed, his face buried in his beer glass. "I'm from way back in the hills of Tennessee. Been tryin' my luck around here, pannin' in those streams out there for the last six months. No luck," he concluded glumly. "They call Leadville the *Silver Queen of Colorado*, but I say somebody else done found all the gold and silver in them hills."

That didn't surprise me. "Not surprised," I said. "People been working these hills pretty hard. What are you gonna do now?"

Holt's beer glass thumped down on the table. "I got skills," he crowed. "I got some skills that can make me some money."

I poured myself a refill. "What kinda skills?" I asked, curious. "I don't know what I want to do, myself."

Holt leaned back and sucked the air into his lungs. "I kin shoot," he announced. "I could shoot the horns off a grasshopper from fifty yards away." He looked at me and reached for his beer again. "Well, almost, anyway. I'm a great hunter."

I stared at him. "Shootin' deer for the miners? For the cafés? How would you make money hunting around here?"

Holt held one hand in the air while he took a big

swallow. "Railroads," he boomed. "Railroads need food all the time to feed those guys layin' the tracks."

I sat back and thought about that one. Railroads were the other thing I had thought about when I came back to Colorado. "You think you could get a job hunting for the railroad," I said, but I was really kinda talking to myself.

"I know I can," he told me. "What about you? Can you hunt? Or track? Or...something? You don't wanna lay the tracks and hammer in the spikes. Trust me on that one. That's nasty hard work."

I sat back and chuckled. "I can hunt," I said. "I grew up around here, put food on the table for the family a lot of times." I thought a little more. "I could scout," I said. "And I've been a deputy sheriff for the last couple of years."

Holt's hand thumped down on the table so hard I jumped. "That's it!" he boomed. "That's yore ticket! You can scout ahead and keep an eye out for the Injuns. You can help me hunt, an' if they have any trouble with the track layers getting' rowdy, you kin bust their heads!" He stopped with his beer glass halfway to his mouth and looked at me over the top of it.

"You had to bust some heads as a deppity sheriff, right?"

I rubbed the knuckles on my right hand. The soreness was just going away after my dustup with Lunk several days ago, back in Fredericksburg. "I busted my share of heads," I assured him.

The beer glass thunked down on the table. "Let's

you an' me go git a job with the railroads!" Holt thundered.

I held up both hands in the air. "Slow down!" I said. "Where do you go to do this? I don't see any tracks getting laid around here, and I just rode into town on the railroad. Where are they laying the tracks?"

Holt had himself a full head of steam going now. "Durango!" he exclaimed. "We've just got to ride down to Durango an' get a job! They're laying tracks from Durango over to Silverton. There's a bunch o' mining out in Silverton." The huge smile dropped off his face for just a minute. "We'd have to keep the Utes off their backs, maybe. They're a little riled about the railroad goin' through there."

"Let's pull up on those reins a little," I grinned. Holt's excitement was gettin' me pretty fired up, I have to admit. "What's this about Utes getting riled? Have they got the war parties out?"

"Nah, not yet." Holt shook his head back and forth a few times. "The Ute chief is pretty peaceful. Name is Ouray, from what I've heard, and he's smoked the ole peace pipes a few times. It's them war parties you have to worry about once in a while. Guy named Seva-something or other, he's got 'em stirred up a time or two."

I was pretty sure Holt's backwoods accent had turned that Ute's name into something his own mama wouldn't recognize. I figured he knew what he was talking about, though. He'd been out there working a claim for six months.

"What about now?" I said, leaning forward. "Are they riled up right now?"

Holt shook his head again. "Not so's you'd notice," he said. "They're pretty peaceful out there where the rails are goin' in. A guy named Meeker's got 'em a little stirred up, but it ain't that close to where the rails are. Just got to be careful. We're running that railroad across what was allus their land. Some of 'em don't like it much."

I sat back and thought it over. All in all, it sounded like a way to get my feet on the ground and make some money. I looked over at the bar. That waitress girl seemed like she might be watching me. What was that about?

I looked back at Holt. "You said we've got to go down to Durango to see about a job," I reminded him. "Is there a train to get us there?"

Holt shook his head. "Yeah, I guess, but we could ride our hosses down there. It'll take about a week, but it's some pretty country." He tipped back the last of his beer. "Are we pards?"

We shook hands on it and agreed to meet at the livery stable the next morning. Holt had some business to take care of, so we agreed to meet at ten o'clock.

I was on my way out when I heard my name. I turned around and saw the pretty waitress who had served us. Holt turned around and gave me an elbow in the ribs. "I think she likes you, bubba. Maybe she's done set her cap for you."

I ignored Holt and watched the girl as she walked

over. She seemed pretty nervous. I took my hat off and waited for her to talk.

"Mr. Smith," she said. "Sorry, I wasn't trying to listen in on you, but I heard you say your name is Latigo Smith."

"Right," I said awkwardly. "Call me Lat." I turned my hat over in my hands a few times. "What can I do for you, Miss?" I cussed myself out in my head for sounding so stiff.

"Joanna," she said, holding out her hand. "Joanna Locke."

Her hand felt downright tiny in mine, but she was even purtier up close, I got to say. I heard Holt snorting back there behind me, so I shifted a little to block him from her view. This was complicated enough already.

"I need to talk to you about something," she said.

"Joanna! Joanna!" came a voice from across the room. "Got some boys that need some beer over here!"

I looked over her shoulder. Mustache, back there behind the bar, was barking at her. He looked a little lathered up.

She turned around to look at him, then turned back to me, her face a little red. "Can't talk now," she said, glancing back over her shoulder. "Could we meet here, maybe nine o'clock in the morning? I really need to talk."

"Sure," I said. "Glad to." I looked at the bar. Mustache had taken a couple steps in this direction. I glared at him. He backed off a little. "Tomorrow mornin'," I said and pushed out the doors.

Holt was snickering out on the boardwalk.

"Oh, shut up," I told him. "See you at the livery stable tomorrow."

Joanna Locke counted the money in her pocket as she left the Whiskey Wagon. As usual, it was a mixture of coins and small nuggets. There was a trading post down the street where she traded the nuggets for money about once a week. She was getting pretty good at guessing how much the nuggets were worth. Tonight, it looked like she'd had a pretty good day with the tips.

She reached her room at the boarding house, just a few blocks down the street, went to her room, and lit a lantern. She sat on the bed, rubbing her feet. That was the hardest part about being a waitress. She was on her feet all day.

Joanna looked at a faded photograph on her dresser. The picture was her best memory of her mother. She knew they had taken it at a place called Cherry Creek when she was still a baby. They had come west in covered wagons, and Joanna had been born on the trail. The original goal, she knew, had been California, but the trip was too hard on a new mother with a baby.

Her parents had stopped at a bend in the South Platte River near a place called Cherry Creek. A few years later, the name was changed to Denver City and then Denver. Joanna had grown up near there.

Her mother had rallied for a few years after they'd stopped and settled down. Her dad said she had gained strength and looked better for several years, then began fading away again. Consumption, they called it. Joanna's best memories of her were from the time she was about eight or nine years old.

Her clearest memory came from a talk she'd had just a few weeks before her mother's death. There had been stories for as long as Joanna could remember about her grandfather, a man named Ezekiel Dunne. Ezekiel had been a fur-trapping old mountain man in the west. Joanna was sure that the stories from her mountain man grandfather Ezekiel had fueled her mother's desire to come west.

Her favorite story was the one about the black rocks that turned out to be gold when the rocks were assessed in Los Angeles. Black rocks gathered on a mesa top back when Ezekiel was running from the Utes with his partner, somebody named Barnabus Smith. Joanna had memorized how the story went— they could never find more of the gold. The mesa top was about three days out of Fort Uncompahgre, which no longer existed. The mesa was one of three in a row, and it was the tallest one, in the middle.

It wasn't much to go on. Barnabus Smith had died without finding it. Ezekiel Dunne had died a few years later, leaving just his daughter and his granddaughter, Joanna. Barnabus Smith had a nephew named Latigo, supposedly running around Colorado somewhere. Nobody had seen him in years.

The clear memory from a few weeks before her

mother's death was about the black rocks and old Ezekiel Dunne. Joanna smiled at the memory. It was her mother's favorite story.

"Your father doesn't think much of the story about your grandfather and the gold," she had whispered, pulling Joanna in close. "He's a good man, and he works hard. I love him for that." She had stopped and sighed. "He doesn't like the gold story because he doesn't like to take chances or to act on dreams. That's where we're different."

Her mother had pulled back and looked Joanna in the eyes. "We have a hard life, but it's not a bad one," she said. "I can't complain. Your father never wanted to look for that mesa, so we never did. He won't want you to do that, either, but it will be your choice. If it's out there and you can find it, it could change your life. If you can't find it, or there's no more gold there, what have you really lost?"

After her mother passed, her father had raised her. He was a good, hard-working man, as her mother said, farming his land and making a living for the two of them. Joanna had never talked about her mother's favorite story. She knew how much it would upset him. When he passed two years ago, she had sold the farm and moved to Leadville. It was a boom town with some opportunities. She had worked, saved her money, and kept her ears open for anything about black rocks and gold.

She had learned how it could happen. Gold, exposed to moisture and the scorching sun, could turn a dark color. Had someone mined ore up there, or carried it up, then abandoned and lost it? She didn't know. Leadville miners were doing well, but only a few of them had heard much about gold nuggets turning black. Mostly, they knew about black stuff in the sluice boxes. That meant silver.

The trail had grown cold here. Joanna had bought maps. She knew Fort Uncompahgre was long since abandoned and torn down. They had built it where the Gunnison and Uncompahgre Rivers met. Three hours in a southwesterly direction might put her somewhere east of Silverton. She had some money saved now but didn't know how to proceed. She wasn't even sure if she wanted to proceed. Maybe her father was right.

Today, though, she had heard the name Latigo Smith. He'd shown up in the Whiskey Wagon out of nowhere. True, there were many people named Smith running around, but there couldn't be too many Latigos. Had he ever heard the story? Did she want to tell him about it? Could she trust him?

Joanna didn't feel sure about the answer to any of those questions. She just knew she wanted to talk to him. If he'd never heard of it and thought she was crazy, she could just walk away. No harm done. What could it hurt to ask about it? Besides, she thought, he was pretty handsome. Joanna grinned in embarrassment. She would just ask about the mesa and the gold. She had to trust him that much.

I was a little early for the meeting with Joanna. I paced back and forth in front of the Whiskey Wagon, sniffing the smells wafting across the street from a café, doing some good business this morning. I was staring into the café when a voice behind me made me jump.

"Hungry? We can go over there and I'll buy breakfast."

I wheeled around and saw Joanna standing behind me. Where, I wondered, had she come from?

She laughed and started across the street. "Come on," she said. "I used to work in there and the owner gives me free breakfast about half the time."

I followed her across the street and into the Hoot' n' Holler café. The owner, an older guy with an accent I couldn't quite figure out, made a big fuss over Joanna and took us to a table in the corner. Ten minutes later, I tucked into eggs, bacon, potatoes, and toast. I glanced up once in a while to see Joanna watching and smiling. It was too late to worry about whether I was making a pig of myself.

After I had destroyed the food and come up for air, we had a cup of coffee, and Joanna told me what she was thinking about. She started out with a story about her mother and grandfather, a man named Ezekiel Dunne. She got around to the part about black rocks that turned out to be gold, and I just sat and stared.

Joanna stopped and tried to read my face. "My grandfather's partner was a man named Barnabus Smith," she said. "I thought it might be your..." Her voice trailed off, and she seemed to notice for the first time that I was staring.

I reached over to my hat, which was lying on the

table. I turned it over, felt around for the familiar tear in the lining, and pulled out the old letter to Jed Hardy that Pike Hardy had given me. I pushed it across the table to her and sipped coffee while she opened it and read the letter.

"He was my uncle," I explained. "I guess you had figured out we were related."

She finished the letter, folded it back up, and put it back into my hat. I just waited, wondering what she wanted to do. It had been forty years since old Barnabus Smith and Ezekiel Dunne had found that gold.

She avoided my eyes while she sipped her coffee. She put the cup down and leaned across the table. "I've been here in Leadville for over a year now," she said. "I have talked to a lot of miners." She stopped and chuckled. "Most of them were sober, some not. The story of Barnabus Smith and the black pebbles, or black rocks, is something a few of them have heard of. Many people have looked for that mesa." She looked at my hat, where she had placed that letter. "It sounds like Barnabus Smith went back and looked a few times. Nobody has found it."

She folded her hands on the table and smiled at the waitress while the girl refilled our coffee cups. She leaned forward again. "This is the part where I'm afraid you'll think I'm crazy," she said. "I want to look for that mesa. I want to see if there is any more gold up there."

I hemmed and hawed and kept looking at those blue eyes. I was having trouble telling them no. "I'm leaving this morning," I finally said. "I've found a partner and we're pulling out for Durango this morning."

Joanna leaned across the table and put her hand on my arm. "I have some money saved, and there's nothing keeping me here," she said. "I want to come with you."

THREE
ROAD TO DURANGO

Well, I could explain all the stuff I tried to tell her. How I told her it might not be safe, and I was gonna work for the railroad, not hunt for gold, and how I would be away from Durango most of the time, probably. I tried telling her all that stuff. Fact is, I finally just caved in and told her she could come with us to Durango.

I came out of that Hoot 'n Holler café and saw Holt packing up his horse just across the street. He tied down some gear and waved when I came out. Joanna had stopped to talk to the owner of that café. Holt trotted across the street. He started to talk, but I stopped him.

"You remember that girl that brought us the beer last night, right?" I asked.

Holt grinned big. "Shore do," he said. "She done taken a shine to you."

"Well," I told him, "The thing is, we just had break-fast, and I told her she could come to Silverton with us." I glared at him. "And it ain't 'cause she taken... took a shine to me."

Holt stared past me and saw Joanna, just now coming out of the café. He put his hand on my shoulder and stared at me. "Teach me everything you know, Pard," he said. "I'm gonna learn a lot from you."

Joanna came out and saved me from havin' to explain anything else to Holt. I introduced them and said to Joanna, "Holt is my partner. I guess it'll be the three of us riding down to Silverton."

Joanna shook his hand. "I hope you don't mind, Holt," she said. "Lat was nice enough to invite me. I can do all the cooking," she offered. "And I'm a good shot with my Winchester, too."

Holt took her hand and bent over it like he was a duke in somebody's castle or somethin'. He took off his hat and kissed her hand. "You are shore welcome, ma'am," he said. "Didn't neither one of us want to do the cookin'. I kin shoot all the food we'll need, but it don't never hurt to have another gun if we need it." He put his hat back on and I thought he was gonna take a bow or something, but he quit before he got to that.

Joanna went to the Whiskey Wagon to tell Mustache she wouldn't be coming back to work. I think she was gonna enjoy doing that. Holt was finishing up packing, so I went down to the livery stable to get my horse.

I paid the livery stable charge and was about to lead my horse out when I saw the old guy that ran the stable dive into an office in the corner of the place.

That didn't seem right. I looked around and saw a couple guys come into the livery, and I knew they were trouble right away. They spread out and started toward me, eyeing my horse an' sizing me up.

I stood there and watched them walk across the yard. I could smell the hay and manure as I moved just slightly to get the sun out of my eyes. It was filtering through the cracks in the livery stable boards. They were probably counting on me being a little blinded by it. My horse, a chestnut gelding I'd bought down in Fredericksburg, stomped his hoof behind me. Things seemed to slow down while they moved in.

From the corner of my eye, I could see Joanna come out of the Whiskey Wagon and start toward the livery stable. She stopped when she saw what was happening. I knew she was watching, and this wasn't gonna be pretty.

My hand dropped to my holster and I rested it there. They glanced back and forth, not so sure of themselves for the first time. Nobody really wants to be looking down a barrel. The one on my left looked like the most trouble. He was a little older and had a nasty scar running down the side of his face. His hand hovered near his right-hand gun, but he wore two, tied down. He'd done this before.

The other one was younger and bigger. He was probably the muscle of the two of 'em, I decided. He'd probably rather settle things with his fists and his boots. Guns were going to settle this one, though. I shifted slightly to face the older one. He noticed it and took a half-step back.

"Nice horse, mister," he said. He stared at me

without blinking. Reminded me of a lizard. Big lizard, but still a lizard.

"I'm kinda partial to that horse myself," I said. "He ain't for sale, just in case you boys were wondering."

The gun hand laughed, but it finished up with a wheezing, raspy cough. "Wasn't thinkin' about buyin' nothing," he said.

His eyes flickered, and I palmed the Colt and fired just as soon as I saw the flicker. The eyes give it away every time. My first bullet drove him back to the rail. The second one slammed him hard against the boards and he slid down slowly, the gun falling from his dead hands.

I wheeled toward the second one. His hands were in the air, and I could see they were shaking. This wasn't his kind of fight, and he wanted none of it.

"Ease off that gun belt, son," I told him. "Drop it on the ground, step back from it, and keep those hands where I can see 'em. Nobody else needs to die today."

Now I think ordinarily one or two gunshots in a town like Leadville wouldn't have gotten the sheriff's attention. He had too much to worry about as it was. This early, though, I heard the door to the jail and sheriff's office slam shut behind me. I shifted a little so I could see the sheriff comin' without taking my eye off the kid kneeling in the livery yard. Gunfire in the morning had caught the sheriff's attention. Just my luck.

The gate to the livery opened and closed. The sheriff was holding his Colt on me. That wasn't good. "What happened, Mouse?" he barked.

I looked at the kid on his knees with his hands

behind his head. First off, I couldn't believe they called him Mouse. I wouldn't have put up with that. Second, he started lyin' just as soon as his mouth opened.

"He done started it," Mouse said. He pointed one hand at me and kept the other behind his head.

"Didn't happen that way, Sheriff," I said, easing my Colt back into the holster. "They came after me with an idea of stealin' my horse here."

"He's telling you the truth, Sheriff." We both wheeled a little to see Joanna standing at the gate. "I was walking down the street and I saw the whole thing. Snake, over there, and Mouse jumped him as he was leading his horse out. Snake went for his gun."

My brain was still tryin' to figure out how there could be two people in this world named Snake and Mouse. I shook my head and left off trying. I could still be in some trouble here, being a stranger in town and all.

The old geezer came stumbling out of his office and stood there, looking around at all of us. The sheriff turned to face him.

"What about you, Herb?" the sheriff asked. "Tell me what you seen down here. Who taken a shot at who first?"

Herb scratched himself and shook his head back and forth, mumbling to himself. "Didn't see nuthin', Sheriff," he said finally. "I jest tucked myself into the office back there when I saw there was gonna' be some lead flyin' around this place. Don't need none of that lead in my old hide. Didn't see nuthin'." He shook his head a couple more times and went off to shovel some stalls, still mumbling to himself.

The sheriff growled under his breath and waved his gun at the both of us. "Gimme your gun," he said, picking up Mouse's gun belt from the ground.

I lifted my Colt out carefully and handed it over. He motioned at me to turn around and marched both of us out of the livery stable. I could see we were going to the jail. Already in trouble and I only been here a day, I said to myself. Maybe my momma was right about how I just couldn't stay out of trouble.

"I got me a cell for each of ya while I try to figger things out," the sheriff said. He marched us into the jail and locked each of us up. He stopped outside my cell. "Yore a stranger around here," he observed. "When did you get into town?"

"Yesterday," I said. "Plannin' to ride out today." I knew he would like that part. Sheriffs like to see troublemakers leave town. I remember how that is.

"Jest got here an' you already shot a guy," he growled. "What did ya do before you come to my town?"

"Came in from Texas," I said. "I was a deputy sheriff in a town called Fredericksburg down there. You can send a telegram and check with Sheriff Pike Hardy if you want."

His eyebrows shot up, and he backed off a step. "Hmmph," was all he said. "We'll see about that."

I didn't hear a thing from the sheriff for the next half hour except for his talking to himself and opening and closing a few drawers. Then I smelled some coffee brewing. Probably doesn't know what to do, I thought.

I heard the door open and close out front, then I heard Joanna's voice.

"You'll want to look at this, Sheriff," I heard her say.

The sheriff's voice was suspicious, and he sounded a little peeved. "Where'd you get this?" he barked.

"Over at the post office," she answered. "They had one up on the wall, but they gave me an extra to bring over here and show you. Snake was a wanted man."

Now the sheriff sounded kinda defeated but still a little peeved. I wondered if he had one of those posters shoved in a desk drawer somewhere. "Is that yer boyfriend in there?" he snarled.

"Never saw him before yesterday. I served him beer over in the Whiskey Wagon. I just thought you needed to know about this. And I thought I should tell you what I saw."

The door opened and closed, then it got quiet again. I took a seat on the bunk in my cell again and waited. The sheriff came back after another half hour and opened my cell.

"I'm gonna let you go," he announced. "I don't know nuthin' about that deppity sheriff stuff and I ain't sure I believe it." He stopped and stared at his boots. "Turns out that Snake was wanted for murder, so I guess I'll believe what the girl said."

We passed by Mouse's cell. He came over to be let out, but the sheriff waved him back. "I'm gonna let this one git outta town," he said, "then I'll let you go, mebbe by mornin'. I don't want no more trouble."

He picked up my Colt and gave it back to me, then glared at me. "How soon can you get outta town?" he asked.

I thought for just a minute. "Mebbe two hours," I

said. "I've got to pack up a few things and probly buy me a pack horse at the livery an' get some supplies at the general store. Then I'll be gone."

"Okay," he said gruffly, then stopped me at the door. "Wait," he commanded.

He opened a desk drawer and fumbled around inside the drawer for a minute, then came over and slapped fifty dollars into my hand. "Snake was wanted for murder," he explained. "Had fiddy dollars on his head, he did. So that's your'n."

I said nothing, just let myself out. He would just be happy to see me leave. I kinda knew the feeling. Sheriffs don't like to have troublemakers in town, and it had only taken me a day to kill somebody. I shook my head and walked toward the livery stable. I'd lost track of how many men I'd shot now.

Herb gave me the fisheye when I came back to the livery stable, but he led my horse out for me. I looked around the stable. "How much for a packhorse?" I asked. "He won't have to carry too much, just some vittles, mainly."

Herb scratched himself, then left and came back with an old horse. I walked around him and checked his teeth. He still had some miles in him and could do what we wanted, I thought. I pointed at the horse. "How much?"

Herb sucked at his teeth and stared off into the distance, doin' some ciphering in his head, I guess. He shoved his hands in his pockets and looked me in the eye for the first time today. "One-fiddy," he said.

"He's old," I pointed out. "I'll bet you paid a lot less for him than that. One-twenty."

Herb looked injured and took a step back. "Why don'tcha jest pull that Colt on me, too?" he whined. "Yore tryin' to stick me up."

I grinned, and we got down to haggling over that old packhorse. We settled on one-thirty-five, plus a small bait of grub for the horses. Herb might have got the best of me, I thought as I left the livery. I led the horses down to the general store and tied them to the rail.

I bought some flour, beans, dried fruit, and some ammo. The rest of the food we would have to shoot on the way. The shopkeeper had a hand-drawn map of the area from here to Silverton, so I bought that, too.

I loaded up my purchases on the packhorse and led both horses over to my boarding house room, where I found both Holt and Joanna waiting for me. I settled my bill and had my bag on the packhorse in no time.

I swung aboard the chestnut and looked at them. "I've got a map and a little food," I told them. "Ready to hit the trail?"

Holt looked at the Whiskey Wagon, then checked the sun overhead to see what time it was.

"Can't do it," I told him. "Sheriff wants me out of town on account I shot a guy at the livery stable this mornin'." I glanced over at Joanna. "I mean, he was an outlaw, and he went for his smokewagon first, but I sure enough shot him," I said.

Holt nodded sadly and swung aboard his horse. "Can't be helped, I guess," he agreed.

Joanna mounted up and fell in behind me as I led the way out of town. The sheriff was on the front porch of the jail, watching. He tipped his hat as we rode past. We moved on out of Leadville and struck the trail for Durango.

———

Mouse was in a foul mood by the time the sheriff let him out of jail the next morning. There'd been nothing but a plate of beans last night and no breakfast this morning. And he was the one who didn't even pull his gun, he growled to himself.

The sheriff handed Mouse his gun belt on the way out. He reached for the belt, then the sheriff pulled it back and gave him a hard stare. "Don't even think about trying to catch up with that feller and pick a fight," the sheriff warned. "Snake was a pretty fair hand with a gun, from what I've heard, and it don't look to me like he even cleared the leather. Took two, right through the chest. That's a dangerous man."

Mouse hadn't really thought about a gunfight, but he'd been having some ideas about knocking the guy down and putting his boots to him. That was more like what Mouse was good at. He took his gun belt and pushed past the sheriff without a word.

"Mouse! One more thing."

He paused at the door and looked around.

"You and Snake wasn't nothing but trouble when you was in town. Snake is headed for boot hill today, an' I want you out of town, too. How soon for you to git outta here?"

Mouse stared back and thought things over. He decided not to try his hand against the sheriff. He swallowed hard and thought. "I got to git me some breakfast," he snarled. "You ain't fed me nuthin' but beans. Then I got to get my stuff together. This afternoon sometime, I guess."

"Noon," the sheriff said. "I'll give you till noon."

Mouse stalked down the street to the café, ordered himself some breakfast, and sulked while he gulped down some coffee. Somebody needed to pay for what had happened, he decided. Needed to pay for the fact that his partner Snake was dead and Mouse had spent the night in jail. That stranger, that's the one that needed to pay.

Mouse tied into his breakfast and thought things over a little more. The stranger—Mouse didn't know his name—had told the sheriff he was gonna leave town and go to Durango. That worked out. Mouse was planning to go to Durango. Even before the sheriff kicked him out, he was planning on it.

Not that Mouse would come after that stranger with a gun. The sheriff was probly right. Snake had an old partner down in Durango. Dangerous man, Mouse knew. He had to admit he was a little scared of the man. Went by the name of Miller. Mouse had never known him to answer to anything else. Miller was operating out of Durango these days. Something to do with making money off the railroads and the miners. Mouse didn't really need to know more.

Mouse had to admit, he wasn't smart enough to make money on his own. He had to work for somebody else, maybe bustin' some heads or just scarin' people who were slow to pay up. He would see about working for Miller.

Mouse finished eating and left enough money for the meal. On the way out, he saw some money lying on another table and slipped it into his pocket. Mouse could use the spending money. He needed to get down to the general store and get himself a little grub and ammo for the road. He figured he had about an hour.

On the way to the general store, he thought of something that made him smile for the first time today. He would tell Miller about this stranger who shot Snake. Snake and Miller was old partners, right? Maybe Miller would get his revenge for him. Mouse liked the idea.

One hour later, he left Leadville.

FOUR
TROUBLE ON THE TRAIL

W e were two hours down the trail when I called the first halt. It had been a couple years since I had ridden in this part of the country, and I had to take a second to look around me when we stopped to water the horses at a mountain lake. I could see mountain peaks reflecting off the water when I hunkered down to fill my canteen. The smell of the pine trees reminded me of when I was a kid. I glanced over at Joanna and Holt. I guess they were used to this.

Holt had his head up, looking around, and that reminded me we were in Ute country. They were mostly peaceful lately, but that didn't mean all of 'em would feel that way. I cocked my head a little and looked down the trail. We would be in some narrow passes betwixt some rocky ledges and such within a day. We'd best have a sharp lookout in places like that.

Joanna was quiet and had kept to herself all day, and that downright puzzled me. She hadn't been that way when I met her. I wondered if she had changed her mind about coming to Silverton. Too late to turn back by the time we made camp the first night. Holt and I would be pushing on without turning back.

We made camp in a meadow just to the side of a mountain stream that gave us water for the horses and our canteens. Holt dropped a doe at dusk and we set to work cleaning the deer. We could take enough venison with us to feed the three of us for a few days. Joanna got a fire going, gathered some wild onions, and made a stew for us over a small campfire. We put it out right after cooking. No need to invite a war party to join us.

After I had washed out the kettle and tin plates in the stream, I laid out my bedroll next to a fallen log. Joanna watched for a while, then came over and sat on the log next to my bedroll. I took that as a sign it was time for a pow-wow. I sat down next to her on the log. Holt moved away out of earshot and laid out his bedroll near the ashes of the campfire.

Joanna studied my face. "I want to talk a little more about the gold your uncle and my grandfather found," she said. "If you don't want to talk about it anymore, just tell me. I'm grateful to make the trip to Durango with you guys. I just want to tell you a little more about what I know."

I studied my hands in the fading light and thought about it. It seemed like half the country had gone chasing after some lost mine or hidden gold somewhere over the years. There were more stories about such things than you could shake a stick at. My uncle had found some gold, I guess, but when he went back to find more of it, it wasn't there.

She waited while I thought about it. Finally, I looked over and nodded. "We can talk about it," I said, "but I'm not making any promises about helping you look for it. I came to get me a good start in this country. I need more at the end of the trail than old stories and empty pockets."

She grinned and reached over like she was gonna pat my arm, then thought better of it. "I understand," she said. "My mother used to talk about the black pebbles all the time. After a while, they were black rocks." She chuckled. "I guess they got bigger after the story got told a few times."

I smiled and relaxed a little. It was nice to hear her laughing. It was the only sound out here besides a few bird calls and a little gurgle from the stream.

"You showed me the letter from your Uncle Barnabus," she said. "Do you know anything else about the story?"

I shook my head. "I'd never heard a thing about this until I was ready to leave Texas," I said. "I didn't set much store by it and didn't really figger on looking for it. I only kept the letter because it's just about the only thing I have to remind me of my family."

"Same for me." She shifted a little on the log to look me in the face. "About reminding me of family, I mean. I took a chance talking to you about this," she said. "I don't know much about you, but trying to find that mesa by myself is something I can't do. We have the most in common on this subject. It was family for both of us."

She stopped to see how she was doing. I think she could tell from my face I still wasn't much in favor of traipsing around hundreds of square miles in Colorado. We'd be looking for something that might not even be there.

She kept going. "Here's what I know," she told me. "They left Fort Uncompahgre, which isn't there anymore. It was where the Gunnison River and the Uncompahgre Rivers meet. They were three days out, headed for Los Angeles. A war party of Utes chased them. They climbed the mesa, which was the tallest of three mesas in a row. They found the gold up there."

I picked up a stick, fetched out my knife, and whittled. It's what I like to do when I'm trying to think. The shavings flew for a while. She just watched me until I put away my knife and tossed away the stick.

"Okay," I said, "I didn't know the part about three mesas in a row and so on. That might help a little. Lots of stuff we still don't know, though. Three days out, a hundred miles, whatever it is—how fast they were riding can make a big difference. How long were they running from the Utes? We don't know. *Riding on a line* could mean lots of things."

I stopped and slid down to the ground so I could lean back against the log. Joanna did the same thing. "Were they trying to avoid war parties? That might mean they weren't quite on a line to the southwest. Did they have to avoid rivers that had gone over their banks? Were they trying to avoid climbing over the tallest peaks out there?"

I shook my head and glanced over. She looked so sad. I think I caved a little again. "Here's what I'll do," I said. "Holt and I want to get a job layin' tracks from Durango to Silverton. We might cover some of that ground. I'll keep my eyes open while I'm huntin' and scoutin' and such. I'll let you know if I see anything. If I find the gold, I'll share it with you."

I held out my hand. She shook it, then leaned in and gave me a big hug. That was nice, I ain't sayin' it wasn't. Still didn't know about huntin' for those black rocks, though.

"I think you're a good man," she said, then went to get in her bedroll.

I stared up at the moon for a minute, then shook my head. "I'm a blame fool, that's what I am," I said. Then I rolled up in my blankets and stared up at the stars. I had another idea about that gold, but I decided to keep it to myself for now.

Day five of our trip to Durango started out like the rest. The sun peaked out over the mountains to our east. Joanna had the coffee and bacon going by the time I peeled off the blankets and took my coffee cup over to the fire. Holt claimed he didn't snore, but I saw him scare off a squirrel or two most mornings with that awful racket.

I sat down on a rock and thanked her for the coffee she handed me. She noticed I took it with my left hand and avoided looking into the fire, even though there was some daylight filtering in already. I still didn't want my eyesight dimmed by staring at the light. She glanced down at my gun belt. I had buckled it on first thing.

Joanna sat down next to me. "You're a careful man, aren't you Lat?" she observed.

I nodded, set the coffee down, and reached for the plate of bacon she offered. "Learned pretty early on I had to be," I told her. "I guess some of us have to grow up a little sooner than others."

"Me too," she said. "I mean, I had to grow up a little sooner." She looked over at Holt, who showed some signs of coming to life.

"What have you done besides help me move to Durango? You didn't seem to have any trouble dealing with that gunman back in Leadville."

I shrugged. "I've done a little bit of everything, I guess," I told her. "I've done a little ranch work, panned for silver and gold a little, worked in a livery stable and a saloon. Even spent the last year as a deputy sheriff down Texas way."

That last one surprised her. "Really? Why did you come back to Colorado?"

I had to think about how to put it into words. "It was good down there," I said. "Good people, a sheriff who saw good things in me and helped me grow up some. Thing is, it wasn't home. It wasn't this." I waved my hand at the trees around us and the meadow in front of us.

She nodded thoughtfully. "I get that," she said. "What did you do in the saloon? I've spent the last six months working in a saloon, and I'm going to look for something else."

"Yeah," I agreed. "Not a good place for ladies most

nights." I thought for a minute. "I did a little of every-thing. I was only about twenty. I mopped up, served a few drinks if they didn't ask for anything besides beer or whiskey. Threw out the rowdies when I had to."

She grinned. "What if the rowdies got rowdy with you?" she asked. "What happened then?"

"Well, I taken...took a few punches. Gave as good as I got, though, and learned some things. Mostly, when I threw 'em out, they stayed out."

She laughed again, then got up to reach for the coffeepot. Holt had rousted himself out of the blankets, stomped into his boots, and was headed our way, yawning and scratching himself and holding out his coffee cup. Time to start another day.

We found ourselves on some narrow trails as we moved along today, moving through deep valleys and canyons. There were rocky cliffs on either side of us, and from time to time, we could hear a waterfall or rushing stream.

We moved out at the bottom of a switchback, and it took me by surprise to see a camp set up in the valley below us. I threw up my hand to stop Joanna and Holt and stared down into the valley. My stomach flipped over a time or two when I saw it was a Ute camp.

A few of them emerged from the tipis down below and stared up at us. They seemed curious more than anything, and I could see a lot of women and children. An old man walked to the edge of their campsite and stood staring at us.

My stomach settled down a little. This for sure wasn't a war party, it was a traveling band of Utes with women and children, maybe moving a little farther up to higher valleys now that the weather was warming. I studied the trail in front of us, it would take us around the camp, not directly through it.

We started forward again. I waved at the old man. He stood there for a minute, then went back to get his pony. I could see he was going to meet us down below on the trail.

I only knew a word or two of the Ute language. I checked with Holt and Joanna—they knew less about the Ute language than me. Luckily, I knew the word for *peace*. I planned to use that.

The old man was at the side of the trail when we came down into the meadow. He stood looking at us. He lifted a hand and stood still, the wind blowing the feathers in his hair. He looked at me and said something in Ute I didn't understand.

I lifted a hand in the air and said *peace*. He smiled for just a second. I felt sure he understood me. A few kids came running toward us from the camp. He turned and barked a few words at them, and they retreated to the camp. Clearly, this was the guy in charge around here.

He turned back to look at me and said something else I didn't understand. He pointed, and I guessed he wanted to know where we were going. I pointed down the trail in front of us and said the word for *village*. I hoped he could understand me because I was all out of words. This was gonna be one short powwow.

He nodded and stood back, then lifted his hand toward the trail in front of us. I lifted a hand in what I hoped was a friendly wave, and we all moved past.

We moved around the bend and I risked a glance behind me. Nobody was following.

___

By day nine of the trip, we found more barren landscape, rocky slopes, and scree-covered hillsides. We were all getting pretty eager to get to Durango. I hadn't forgotten about the possibility of highwaymen out here—they had operated in this area for a while, robbing miners of hard-won gold dust and pebbles. I was hoping the only adventure we would have on this trip would be the Ute camp.

That's what I get for thinking. We skirted a foothill and rode past an abandoned campsite. I pulled up to take a look, wondering how long it had been since somebody had camped here. I started to dismount to check the ashes at the campfire site when Joanna stopped me with a hand on my arm.

Three men rode out of a stand of pine trees. They had bandannas over their faces and their hats pulled low, so there wasn't too much doubt about what they wanted. We spread out a little, and I saw Joanna slip her double-barreled shotgun out of her scabbard. She slid it quietly across her lap.

The one on the left looked like he was in charge. He rode out to me, holding a pistol on my belly. "We'll take yore cash money and valuables," he announced.

I looked at him and glanced over his shoulder. The other two had stayed farther back. Both had drawn their pistols, but they weren't paying much attention to Joanna and Holt. One of them glanced back over his shoulder at the stand of pines they'd come from. I eased my feet out of the stirrups, then leaned over and spit.

"I don't think so," I told him. "We ain't got many valuables, but were kinda partial to them."

He spurred his horse several steps closer and waved his pistol at me. "We got the drop on you," he told me. "Three on three, but one of you'uns is a girl."

I looked over at Joanna. "She's a girl, all right," I said. "But she's got a shotgun with two barrels. Hard to miss with a shotgun this close. Hurts, too, if you're gut-shot." I looked back into the trees where they'd been hiding and raised my voice. "Unless mebbe you've got another one back there in the woods, too yellow to come out face-to-face."

Somebody cursed and rode out of the woods. The guy across from me looked back. He'd been wanting to keep his bushwhacker buddy back there as his ace in the hole. His pistol moved away from me as he twisted in the saddle.

I kicked my horse in the ribs, and he jumped forward. I dove on the outlaw and knocked him from the saddle, coming down on him with all my weight. I slammed his head into the ground. The shotgun boomed, and I heard gunfire, but I didn't have time to look.

He tried to get up, but I held on to his gun hand and swung a right uppercut that started at my waist and finished on his chin. He went down in a heap.

I looked up and saw one man unhorsed and on his knees. The shotgun had done its work. The other two were heading for the trees as fast as they could get there. One was holding his shoulder. Holt's pistol was out—he must have exchanged shots and got his man in the shoulder. Joanna had the shotgun up and was tracking them. She never needed the second barrel.

I took the pistol from the guy I had knocked out, then grabbed his rifle from his horse. I put them both on our packhorse. I checked the guy on the ground who'd taken the shotgun blast—he might make it, but he would be hurtin'.

I came back to the first guy. He was holding his jaw and trying to get to his feet. "Stay down," I said, "and listen to me." He tried to stand, and I knocked him down again.

"You don't pay attention," I said. "That's a bad habit. Stay down this time." He glared at me but stayed down. I pointed at the man who'd been unhorsed by the shotgun. "Your buddy over there is hurt. You better see to his needs. I'll leave his pistol but take all but one bullet. Your pistol and rifle are comin' with me."

He started up off the ground, but I cocked my fist and he stayed down. "You can't leave me out here without a gun!" he shouted.

"Your buddy has one. I'd be real choosy with how you use that bullet. As to your pistol and rifle, I've seen how you don't play nice with 'em. I'll make sure they get a good home."

I checked to make sure Joanna and Holt were fine, they were. We left the two outlaws and rode on toward Durango.

Mouse watched the fight from the woods. He had followed these three all the way from Leadville, staying back and out of sight. For one thing, he thought they could draw the fire if they ran across a war party. For another, he used their campsites after they'd left in the morning. Easier to stir up their ashes and make some coffee that way than to build a fire from scratch. He'd had nothing but beans and jerky all the way. No risking a fire for him at night.

As he watched the four men ride out, Mouse stayed back. He had a feeling the attackers had been some of Miller's men, but he didn't know them. It was something else he could tell Miller when he got to Durango.

FIVE
MOUNTAIN RAILS

Durango looked a little more like my kind of place when we rode in after our ten days on the trail. It was busy, but much smaller than Leadville. It didn't feel like I could get my pockets picked just walkin' down the street like in Leadville.

We pulled up to a hitching rail and looked around. The San Juan Mountains rose in the background, and it was a mining town, just like Leadville was. You could see the miners walking along on their day off, along with some guys who were probably railroad workers and a few townsfolk. A lot of wagons were going up and down the street.

I looked over at Joanna. "What do you think of the place?" I asked.

She looked around and smiled. "Feels more like home than Leadville," she said. She pointed at a sign down the street. "Looks like that's where you and Holt want to go," she said.

I looked where she was pointing. Past a general

store, café, and two saloons, there was a hand-painted sign that said: *Railroad Hiring—Apply Within*. I nudged Holt and pointed at the sign. His forehead wrinkled up.

"What's it mean *apply within*?" he asked. "Go inside an' ask for a job?"

"Umm, yeah, there's a little office set up inside there, I guess," I told him.

"Hmmph. okay. Don't know why they can't just say that," he grumped.

We climbed down, and I sniffed the air. "We've been livin' on trail food for eight days," I reminded them. Joanna's a great cook and all, but I can smell coffee and maybe some steak." I tested the air with my sniffer again. "And maybe some pie," I added. I pointed at the café two doors down. "Anybody else for the café?"

Holt swung around and started for the café. "Jest try and stop me, pard," he said. Joanna took my arm, and we went in.

Joanna settled into a chair next to me, and we all ordered some food. When the server left, Joanna asked if either of us had ever worked for a railroad. We shook our heads at the same time.

"There were mostly miners in the Whiskey Wagon," she reminded us. "But railroad workers came through sometimes. They liked to talk to the girls, and they told me a few things about the railroad work. I could tell you what I know before you go down there."

"We're all ears," Holt told her. "And I've got me some big ears. Shoot."

Joanna chuckled and stopped for a second when they brought her coffee. "The hardest job sounded like the guys who have to actually carry the rails and lay the track," she said. "I think they made the least money, too. Guys like engineers make the most, probably. They're working with some steep climbs and canyons. Then there's the guy that sets up the dynamite. Sometimes they had to blast through the rock. That's the most dangerous thing, I think. Weather is a problem for all of them in the winter."

Holt heaved a sigh and sucked down half his coffee with one slurp. "That's sounds downright discouragin'," he said. "Tell me some good news."

Joanna grinned. "I think you guys have the right idea," she said. "People with special skills don't have to lay the track and can make a little more money. You were talking about hunting for food and scouting. She looked at me. Those railroad camps are like a little moving town. Maybe they could use an ex-sheriff."

"How much?" I asked. "We might need to know how much to ask for."

Joanna shrugged. "Those guys got a little drunk and probably said they made more than they did, but I think track layers make maybe a dollar-fifty a day. People with skills or special jobs, two dollars might be more like it."

I noticed some guys looking at Joanna while we ate. Even after eight days on the trail, she was a pretty lady. My ma used to tell me not to let the grass grow under my feet. I was never quite sure what she meant by that, but I figured this could be one of those times when the grass was growin'. Going off to work for the railroad and all, I just didn't quite know what to do about it.

She caught me looking at her sideways and smiled. "What?" she asked.

My brain commenced to scrambling around for what to say, and it was work, let me tell you. "Er, what about you?" I finally asked. "You didn't want to work in a saloon anymore. What do you want to do around here?"

"Bakery," she said. "We passed one when we first got to town. I'm surprised you boys didn't lead the charge into that place. Miners, cowboys, railroad workers, anybody who has had no home cooking likes the bakeries. They had a hiring sign in the window. I'm going down there."

―――

We parted ways in front of the café, and Holt and I made our way down to a ramshackle-looking office where they were hiring railroad workers. The office was more like a half-built office with a tent over the top. We pushed inside and found a man built like a barrel, puffing away on a pipe. His face lit up when he saw us.

"Got me a couple o' prime track layers, right here, I do! My name is Deacon! Step forward and sign up, boys! One dollar-fifty American per day an' all you can eat." He rolled an eye at Holt. "We jest might lose some money on you, son, with that eatin' thing."

Holt gave me an injured look. "He thinks we're track layers, don't he?"

"Sounds like what he said," I agreed. "Sounds like he thinks you can do some damage at the supper table, too. He might be right about that," I observed.

The man at the beat-up old desk blew a thick cloud of pipe smoke into the air. "Got me a couple clowns here, do I?" he sighed. "Okay, boys, if you ain't track layers, tell me why you come into this-here office."

Holt swung his eyes around the room. "Office, you're callin' this? Huh. Well, anyway, I can shoot anything on four legs. Whaddya feed them boys when they've done worked up an appytite all day long?"

Deacon squinted through the smoke and blew another cloud at us. "Anybody kin shoot a buffler," he said. "You jest got to lie on yer belly an' pull the trigger."

"Ain't many buffler left," Holt barked. "Most of 'em been shot for hides and feedin' other railroad workers an' such. You need somebody can track and shoot deer and elk and other game. I'm your man." He looked over at me. "Him, too. Me and him are in on this together."

Deacon turned his eyes to me. "You a scouter and hunter, too? Where have you done any scoutin'?"

"I did some growing up, right here in these mountains," I said. "Hunted me some deer an' elk, put food on the table. Did some scoutin' for the army. I also done some scouting down Texas way. Was a deputy sheriff down there."

Deacon's feet came down from the table and he looked me over carefully. "Deppity sheriff, huh? You have to knock some heads sometimes, get in a few knuckle-and-skull fights?"

I nodded.

Deacon leaned forward. "Ever have to shoot you some outlaws?"

I nodded again. "A couple times," I said.

Deacon leaned back and thought things over, still puffing away on that worn-out pipe. Eventually, he came to a decision and leaned forward.

"Okay, you boys are hired," he said. He pointed at Holt. "You kin be the hunter. You kin both do some scouting, but you're the hunter. We'll need a couple deer or mebbe an elk most days. Only takes one of you to pull the trigger, though."

He looked over at me. "You kin do some scouting, like I said. You kin bust some heads, sheriff-like, if some boys get outta line." He stubbed out the cigar and squinted at me. "You kin also check into things if'n some of our supplies go missing every once in a while. Agreed?"

"What about the money?" I asked. "We need more than the track layers, we're doing special jobs."

Deacon snorted and put away the pipe. I figured it would take an hour for that office to clear the smoke out. That's assumin' he didn't pull it out and light it up after we left. "Okay," he said. "Two dollars a day. That's top o' the line money."

Holt looked over at me. I had a feeling this guy might have a real problem with *supplies that go missing*. "We was thinkin' about two-fifty."

Deacon shot straight out of his chair. "Two-fifty!" he moaned. "You think the railroad's made outta gold?"

Neither of us moved. I shrugged and looked at my

hands. "We've got special skills," I observed, remembering what Joanna had said.

Deacon slumped over the desk. "You're holdin' me up with a gun over here," he growled. "Two-twenty-five, that's my best offer."

Holt looked over and nodded. "Done," I said. Deacon pushed a couple of papers at us, we signed them.

"First light tomorrow, be right here," Deacon bellowed as we left. Behind me, I could hear him scratch a match and set the pipe on fire again.

We paused outside and looked at each other. "We got some good money, pard," Holt crowed.

I nodded. "I just wonder how much of a problem he has with stuff going missing," I mumbled. "I might have bit off a lot to chew."

Holt slapped my shoulder. "I'll help ya, pard," he said. He threw back his head and sniffed the air. "I think mebbe I can smell pie at that bakery where Joanna went," he said. "What do you say we go an' check out that bakery?"

Joanna stopped in the street outside a simple little building with plank boards on the side and a roof that tilted just a little. The sign above the door said *Ma's Bakery*. There was a steady stream of customers coming and going. The smell of fresh-baked bread and pies drifted out every time the door opened and closed.

Joanna stepped in and heard a little bell as she

crossed over the threshold and shut the door. Two men, miners by the look of them, were counting out some money to a lady behind the counter. Joanna looked around and saw more plank boards like the ones on the side of the bakery. Ma must have used the extra boards to make shelves to hold her bread, pies, and cakes. A fire blazed in a brick oven behind a worn countertop. Two loaves of bread were baking on the grill that covered the fire.

The two miners walked past her and left the room. A round, tired-looking woman of about fifty years stepped out from behind the counter, wiping her hands on her apron. Flour was sprinkled on her face and gray hair.

"What can I get ya, honey?" she asked, in a not-unkind voice.

Joanna stepped forward, remembering she had just come in from eight days on the trail. It wasn't the best way to make a good impression, but she was here now. "Your sign in the window says you need help," Joanna said.

The woman's eyes brightened. "Yep, that I do," she answered. She looked Joanna over. "Never seen you around here. You new in town?"

Joanna nodded.

"Ma, just call me Ma. Everybody around here does. You ever do any baking, miss?"

"Joanna. I'm Joanna. I've done some baking at home. Made lots of bread and pies and cakes. I've never worked in a bakery before, but I'm a hard worker and I learn fast."

Ma looked at her closely, then slowly nodded her

head up and down. "Well, I surely do need the help, Joanna. I'll give you a try." She smiled for the first time. "A pretty girl like you, I'll bet the men will come flockin' down here to buy stuff. Not that they don't already. Can you start now?"

Joanna looked down at her bag and touched her hair. "I just got into town," she answered. "Can you give me a chance to check into a boarding house and clean up a little?"

Ma nodded and pointed out the window. "Best boarding house in town is just two doors down. Tell 'em I sent you and they'll make sure they've got a room for you. Come back when you're ready." She turned and went back behind the counter.

━━

We stopped off along the way to put all the horses in the livery, including Joanna's. Then, on the way to the bakery, Holt decided his lust for an apple pie could wait until he'd chased his lunch with a beer. After a beer, the apple pie won out, and we moved down the street.

Now we stopped outside *Ma's Bakery*. We hadn't seen another bakery on our way, so this one had to be it. We stepped inside and sniffed the wonderful smells. A lady stepped up to the counter.

"Is that gonna be two pies or just one, boys?" she asked.

"How much?" Holt asked, his hand diving into his pocket.

"Fifty cents," the lady answered. "Call me Ma."

Holt looked sadly at the change he had pulled out of his pocket. "It's gonna have to be just one," he mumbled.

I handed him two bits. "Make it two," I told Ma.

The door opened and closed behind us, and Joanna came in.

"There you are," said Ma. "I've got an apron for you, and you can start kneading the dough for tomorrow's bread."

Joanna patted my shoulder on the way by. Ma looked at Holt and me, then back at Joanna.

"Just like I thought," Ma said. "She's gonna attract men like flies. Hold on, honey," she said, following Joanna behind the counter. "I'm gonna make more bread dough before you start. Tomorrow might be a busy day."

⸺

Clem Miller was in the dimly lit back room of his Durango saloon called The Rusty Bucket. Miller made a little money from the saloon, but he also used this backroom as his office and hangout for planning his operations. The saloon itself was just small potatoes compared to his overall business. The saloon was the only part that was mostly legal.

Nobody called him anything but Miller. The rumor had gone around that Miller had killed a guy just for calling him Clem. Nobody really wanted to risk his life by calling him anything but Miller.

Today Miller was doing something he almost never did. He was having a meeting with his henchman and actually explaining a few of his plans. Usually, he liked to keep his men in the dark, but Wallace was his right-hand man, so Miller filled him in on a few things now and then. It made Wallace feel important.

There was nobody else in the back room. Miller often let one or two of his boys back there—there was a guy who counted the money and passed it out after counting. Most of the money went to Miller. Miller didn't believe in banks. He had a few dollars buried in a hole behind the saloon. He spent the rest of it. Sometimes he let somebody in the back room besides Wallace if they needed to report on things. Today, it was just Wallace. The smell of whiskey and cigar smoke hung heavy in the air. A server put down the whiskey glasses and scurried out.

Miller squinted through the smoke at Wallace. "How many guys you got ready to go?" he asked.

Wallace stubbed out his cigar and put down the whiskey glass. "Got five, right here in town and ready to go, boss," he said briskly. "Got four more scouting up north of here, gettin' the lay of the land. They should be back and ready in about two days. That makes eight, you said seven or eight men with some bark on 'em. That's what we've got."

Miller nodded. He didn't like to tell anybody they'd done a good job, so he didn't, but he was pleased they were just about ready to make his first move against the railroad. A glance over at Wallace told him the man was dying to know more about the plan. Miller decided maybe he should let him in on a bit.

"The railroad is pushin' out to the east," he

murmured. "They're working on gettin' over the Red Mountain Pass first or somethin' like that. They need more supplies. It's what they need to get over that pass and connect with places beyond. Lots of supplies gonna get sent that way soon. Timber, nails, and such. Even some steel to shore up them rails on the tight turns. We're gonna steal the supplies. Lots of money there."

Wallace's eyes shone with admiration as he reached for his whiskey glass. "I knowed you had yoreself a big plan. We'll make it happen."

Miller nodded. Wallace wasn't as smart as Miller, but the man got things done. He had a brutal side to him that Miller could use. Of course, if push came to shove, Miller was sure he could take out Wallace with either his fists or his gun. He just didn't think he would have to. Wallace got paid well, and he liked what he did.

Wallace thought for a moment longer and his brow wrinkled up. "How we gonna get rid of all that stuff?" he asked. "Timber, nails, and steel, that's all gonna be pretty heavy, hauling it out of some rugged country."

Miller waved his hand in the air. "I got a guy who can help me with it," he said confidently. "Won't be nearly as much trouble as you think, and we'll get good money. And it'll set us up for part two of the plan."

He hadn't planned on sharing this part, but Wallace's open admiration was feeding his ego. "Next thing, that railroad—Denver & Rio Grande—plans on finishing out that line to Silverton. Mebbe in the next year or two."

Wallace nodded. He'd heard that part. He'd figured they could keep stealing supplies as the railroad camp worked to the east.

Miller lit a fresh cigar and blew a smoke ring at the ceiling. "There's lots of competition and fightin' between these railroads," he said. "Denver and Rio Grande Western wants a piece of the pie, too. They want new lines out here too. There's even been guns hired by the railroads to protect their tracks and such." He leaned forward and lowered his voice, even though there was nobody within earshot. "We're gonna get hired."

Wallace thumped his fist on the table. "Love it," he blurted. "Which side we gonna hire out for?"

"Both," said Miller, enjoying the sight of Wallace's jaw dropping open. "We'll attack 'em both and take money from both sides for protection."

There was a sudden thumping at the door, and a man burst through. His jaw was swollen and there were bruises covering his face. Wallace recognized the man as Murphy, the guy he'd sent out with two others to scout the area to the north.

Wallace stared at him, then swung around to look at Miller, who had a thundercloud forming on his face. "This is Murph," Wallace explained. "He's one of 'em I told you I sent north to scout." He swung back around to face Murph. "What're you doing here? What happened to yore face? What happened to the others?"

Murph touched his swollen jaw. It was hard to say his words right now. "We got attacked," he sputtered. "Four of 'em, I think. Cain taken a bullet through his shoulder. We got a doc workin' on him outside of town. Reynolds, the other one, well, he got pretty much cut in two by a shotgun. We buried him on the way back."

Miller was on his feet. His voice was quieter now but a lot scarier. "Git him outta here," he growled at Wallace through clenched teeth. "Find out what happened, Wallace, then you come back and explain it to me."

Murph opened his mouth to say more, but Miller's hand dropped to his gun belt. Murph closed his mouth in a hurry and followed Wallace out of the room.

SIX
SUSPICIONS

I met up with Holt the next morning. We'd only taken rooms at the boarding house for one night since we were starting work on the rail lines this morning. I thought with regret that it would be a while before I could explain to Joanna where we had disappeared to.

Holt was lugging his Winchester and a few boxes of ammunition. We both had bedrolls, and I was taking my Winchester too, of course. I could hear Holt grumbling under his breath. "Shoulda asked about them paying for my ammo," he groused. "Cost me five bucks. Don't know when I'll be back to get more."

"Tell that Deacon guy," I said. "They for sure oughta pay for the ammo."

"Yeah," said Holt. He pulled up and stared. "Ain't that Deacon over there waving at us?"

I looked where Holt was pointing. There were a couple dozen men gathering near the railroad tracks at the edge of town. Deacon was standing to the side near a small table he had set up. He was waving at the two of us, just like Holt said.

We changed course to see what Deacon wanted. He pointed at a map spread out over the table as soon as we got there.

"Gotta explain to you boys what's happenin', seeing as how you've got special jobs," Deacon explained. "First thing we're doing is building the rails up over Red Mountain Pass, just north of town." He pointed in that direction. "Then we'll take the rails east."

I looked at the map, feeling a little confused. I guess it showed in my face.

"Say what yer thinking, Smith," Deacon ordered.

I looked up from the map, thinking I needed to not give things away with the look on my face next time. "Oh," I said, pointing at the map, "I know the rail is going from Durango back to Silverton. Thing is, most rails are comin' in from east to west."

"Yup, that's true," Deacon said. "Thing is, we got a little problem with a thing called the Rocky Mountains. You've heard of 'em. Hard to get rail lines over those things."

I had to laugh. "Yeah, I've been up in 'em a time or two."

Deacon dug into this pocket and came out with his pipe again. He reached into another pocket for the tobacco and set the pipe on fire. I wondered how many times a day he did this. He pointed at Holt.

"Holt, you'll need to get on the train with the boys over there and ride up today. It's only five or six miles, but we'll set up camp there and save the back an' forth every day. You'll start bringing in the game and givin' it to Cookie over there." A big man with a cheerful grin waved when Deacon pointed at him.

He looked at me next. "Lat, it's your choice if you want to go up there first or work from town here for a couple days." His mouth drew down into a scowl. "There's a lot of expensive stuff we use to build up over those passes and around the bends, and we're losin' some of it—well, a lot of it. Your main job is to stop that. If'n you want to get some info in town first, okay, but we need you up there in no less'n two days. Do what you need to do to stop it. That's my orders from the big boys."

I rocked back and forth on my heels while I thought that over. "I'll take the two days in town first," I said. I stared off down the tracks, thinking. "Who are the big boys you talked about?" I asked.

"We got us a district superintendent, shows up ever' couple weeks and gives me orders. I'm the one that runs it from Durango," Deacon answered, looking at me curiously.

"Right," I said. "And have you got a clerk or somebody who can show me the records on the supplies and maybe how much of it has gone missing?"

"Yep," Deacon nodded. He pointed at the shack where he'd interviewed us yesterday. "Most days, he shares that office with me," Deacon said. "You can find him in there today." He stopped and stared at me. "You got any ideas how you're gonna do this yet?"

That seemed like a funny question to me. I started to answer, then stopped and shook my head. "First, I'll find out what I can in town," I said. "I'll know more after that."

Deacon nodded and walked away. Holt looked over at me. "You was thinkin' some things you wasn't saying there, Pard," he said. "What's on yer mind?"

I stared at Deacon's back as he walked away. "One thing I learned as a deputy sheriff," I said, "is not to trust anybody. Well, not to trust 'em completely, anyway, until you know a little about 'em. I don't know anything about Deacon or anybody else around here. So, I didn't want to tell him yet."

Holt's grin spread slowly across his face. "So, you've got an idea you don't wanna tell Deacon about," he chuckled. "I thought mebbe you jest wanted to see that Joanna girl a couple more days before you join the rest of us railroad slaves."

I confess that my face might have turned just a tad red. No use denying it. Holt could pretty much see through me. "Okay," I agreed. "I'll probly check in with Joanna before I leave. Mostly I'm workin', though," I defended myself.

Holt chuckled and hoisted his bedroll and knap-sack over his shoulder. "See you in a couple days, Pard," he said. "You'll be dining on fresh elk when you get there, I promise." He joined the others on the train, and it pulled away.

I decided to check in with the clerk first to see what he knew. I found him right away in the shack where Deacon had interviewed us. He gave his name as Matthew, and he had a clammy handshake. He pointed at a camp chair in the corner.

I started with the basics. I told him I was there to

look into some supplies that kept going missing somewhere between here and the railroad base camp. He nodded nervously and avoided looking me in the eye.

"How often do we get in supplies and materials and such and send them up the line?" I asked.

He shrugged and stared at the wall behind me. "Pretty much every two weeks. Sometimes the trains are a little late, but pretty much every two weeks."

He had a habit of bobbing his head nervously when he talked. I concentrated on ignoring it.

"And," I continued, "do you know right away when things are stolen? I mean, you probably have to put in an order to replace what was taken, right? Who tells you about that, and who do you tell when you've made an order?"

"I tell Deacon when I make an order," came the quick answer. He hesitated over the first question. "I know pretty soon after it happens, I guess, but it depends on when Deacon comes back to town. I guess sometimes it maybe happened a few days before, but Deacon isn't always here to tell me."

"Hmm…yeah, I can see that." I stared thoughtfully at the battered desk between us. "Who else knows about the orders and the robberies, I mean, the things that are taken, when the supplies get taken up to the camp, things like that?"

I was a little worried he could maybe see where I was going with that question, but he didn't seem to be bothered by it. "Only the district manager, Mr. Ward. He only comes through once in a while, but he usually asks about it when he's here. I expect him to come in today sometime," he added.

That surprised me. "He's in town today? If I wanted to meet him, where would I look?"

Matthew leaned back and thought about it. "I've seen him at the café a few times. He uses a boarding house around here, but I don't know which one. Sorry, I've really only seen him at the café at breakfast or supper."

"Okay," I said, "just one more thing for now. What you've told me helps. Do you know where the robberies are happening? At a storehouse in town or between here and the railroad camp? Maybe at the railroad camp?"

"Not in town," he answered quickly. "They're locked up and guarded in town. I think on the tracks in between. Not at the railroad camp, I don't think. Deacon would know more about that, though."

"Thanks." I stood and turned around, then paused for a moment. I thought better of what I was about to ask. This kid was far too nervous to do what I was thinking about asking. He would have to have an order from his boss.

I stepped outside and sucked in a cool breeze coming off the mountains. A glance overhead told me it was mid-morning. Maybe, I thought, the rush at the bakery would be over, and Joanna would have some time to talk to me.

The little bell chimed when I walked in. Joanna was wiping off some tables. The smells of fresh-baked goods made me a little weak in the knees. Now I remembered I hadn't even had breakfast. I tried not to drool when I looked at the things on the counter.

Joanna came over and took me to a table in the corner. Ma appeared from the back. "Now there's a hungry man," she said. "I can make you a whole breakfast if you want. Eggs an' bacon an' fresh-baked bread. Family and friends price. Best in town."

"Done!" I said. Joanna went off and brought me a cup of coffee, then sat down with me at the table. "It's my break time," she explained.

I caught her up to date about what my job with the railroad would be and how it might be a few weeks before I could look around out east for that mesa. I went on to explain about the robberies of materials from the trains.

She looked a little disappointed when I told her I wouldn't go east anytime soon but nodded and watched my face while she listened. "Is this going to be dangerous?"

I waited while Ma deposited my breakfast on the table. She took one look at my face and laughed. "I'll expect you here regular when you're in town," she told me.

"Count on that," I answered.

I looked back at Joanna and thought about her question. "Well, I'm dealin' with robbers, and they don't like to get caught. It sounds like they're organized and taking some expensive stuff, so I'll have to be careful. I'm used to that," I added.

She nodded again and got up to bring me more coffee. "What do you plan to do?" she asked when she took her seat again.

I remembered my manners just in time and swallowed before I opened my mouth with that huge forkful of food. "It depends," I said after some thought. "I need to know exactly where the robberies are happening and if they're in the same place on the tracks every time. And I need to know if they happen right when the fresh supplies and replacement stuff are coming in."

I attacked my breakfast again. Joanna traced a line on the tabletop with her finger. "You want to know if somebody is tipping off the robbers when a new shipment is coming?"

I nodded. "I'll have to get up there to the camp, look around a little, and see if I can get some answers. That reminds me," I told her, "I need to find a Mr. Ward, who is the district manager for the railroad. Have you heard that name?"

She shook her head but waved to get Ma's attention. "Ma, have you heard of a Mr. Ward that works for the railroad?"

Ma pointed at the door. "He's comin' in just now. He don't miss a morning when he's in town." She took his order, then pointed at me. "That young feller works for you now. I can bring your food and coffee over there."

He came to the table and Joanna stood up. "Break's over," she explained. She introduced herself and went back behind the counter.

Ward sat down and stuck out his hand. "Cleo," he said. He looked me over. "What is it you do for me, young man?"

I explained Deacon had hired me to do a little

scouting and to see if I could stop the robberies of supplies and materials.

Ward locked in on me. "Good!" he exclaimed. "What kinda experience do you have for this?"

"Deputy sheriff, down Texas way." He just nodded and kept listening. "I talked to Matthew this mornin', and I want to take a look at the storage here. Then I'll go up to the camp."

"Okay, what're you gonna do up there?"

I told him what I'd told Joanna about finding out where the robberies were happening and whether they happened just as soon as the shipment showed up.

"How's that gonna help you catch these guys?"

I didn't like telling my plans to anybody else ahead of time, but I didn't seem to have much choice here. "I want to have Matthew tell whoever he usually tells about these things that a shipment is coming when it ain't coming. Maybe a really valuable shipment."

Ward's eyes lit up. "You're gonna set a trap. I like it." He sipped his coffee and tore into his muffin. "What can I do?"

Good, I thought, I don't even have to ask. "I want Matthew to send that false report, but I don't think he'll do it just with me telling him. He'd be too nervous about it and might tell somebody else, anyway."

"I'll do it." Ward wolfed down the last of his muffin and finished off his coffee. "I'll do it right now, just the way you said." He stood and leaned over the table. "I told Deacon we needed somebody like you. You need to come to me direct on anything, you do it." He shook my hand again and hurried out.

The bell tinkled behind him when the door swung shut. I wondered what he meant by that last sentence.

I walked over to Joanna. Might as well tell her right now what I'd been thinking about the gold the other day. "About those black pebbles," I started.

She stopped wiping the countertop and paid attention. I tried not to get lost in those eyes. "That black stuff covering the gold, that don't...doesn't happen with pure gold, I know that. It comes from other stuff in the nugget, or maybe from water when it bakes in the sun a long time, right?"

She nodded. "What are you thinking?"

"I don't think it's likely that stuff was dug up at the top of that mesa," I explained. "Maybe, but it's not likely. Not just some pebbles and rocks lying there. You remember how my uncle's letter said Ezekiel had seen some of those pebbles before?"

I could see in her eyes she was following me. She swiped at the counter absent-mindedly a couple times. "You're saying they mined it somewhere else, and maybe everybody's been looking in the wrong place!" she murmured. "Of course! Maybe panned in a river somewhere around there?"

"It's somethin' to think about," I agreed. I patted her hand and left.

Ma stopped me at the door. "Where's that friend of yourn with the enormous appetite?"

I chuckled. "He's up at the railroad camp now, gettin' some money in his pocket and working up that appetite. He'll be here and clean you out just as soon as he's back."

I heard them both laughing as the door swung shut behind me.

The train chugged to a halt, and Holt piled off with the other workers. The guy named Cookie set up a campfire and laid a tree branch across on forked sticks he'd pounded into the ground on both sides. He hung a kettle from the tree branch and opened some giant cans. He poured the contents into the kettle, then started opening several bags.

Holt moaned under his breath. "Beans and bread. And I didn't get me no breakfast this mornin'."

He sighed and did like the others, hunting for a spot to throw his bedroll and knapsack. Then he joined the others in line for lunch. Cookie said the same thing every time somebody complained. First, he pointed at Holt. "He's got to go get us some meat. Somethin' to stick to the ribs. Sooner he gets meat, sooner you get some stew."

Feeling more unpopular by the minute, Holt bolted down the beans and left, chewing on his bread as he went. He grabbed his Winchester and an axe, checking the sun overhead. It was still late morning, he decided. More likely to get an elk at sundown, but he would scout the low valleys and set himself up in a good hiding spot near some water. Maybe he would get lucky before dinner.

It took Holt an hour to find the place he was looking for. He'd gone on foot but was smart enough to take a packhorse from the camp to haul back the meat if he shot anything. It was cool at the foot of a peak, but Holt broke out in a sweat in no time as he shaped a lean-to shelter back in the pine trees, about fifty yards from a mountain stream.

He finished his work and stepped back, moving around the shelter to look from all sides. Satisfied, he walked to the stream, stripped to the waist, and splashed himself off in the water. Drying himself with his shirt, he walked back to the shelter and laid down, positioning the Winchester and finding the best field of fire.

Now he could hear voices. He glanced around to look for the packhorse, it was well off the path in a clump of trees. Holt lay still on the shelter's bottom and listened as the voices drew closer. One sounded familiar.

Deacon! One of them was Deacon. The other voice he didn't know. They drew closer and the man he didn't know spoke first.

"Who is this guy?"

"Just a deppity sheriff from a town you never heard of down in Texas. You know they've been on me to find out about the robberies, you know that."

The first voice spoke again. "What's his name? He any good?"

"Settle down, Wallace. You wouldn't know his name if'n I told it to you."

The voices moved farther away, and Holt couldn't make out what they were saying anymore. He lay on the floor of the shelter and thought about it. Half an hour later, he still couldn't make hide nor hair of it and decided to get on with his hunting. Those boys were probably getting grouchier by the minute back at the camp.

The best thing was to lie here and wait for an animal to come for water, he was sure of that. For two hours, he lay still, watching the mountain stream. In the late afternoon, he got what he was waiting for. A four-point elk came to the stream, looked around, and lowered his head for a drink.

Holt shifted to get him in the sights, exhaled slowly, and squeezed off the shot. The buck jumped once and fell. Holt climbed out of the shelter and pulled out his cleaning knife. He still had time to get the meat back for dinner.

As for the few things he'd heard from Deacon and some guy named Wallace, Holt decided to wait until Lat Smith got to camp. He would tell Smith about it then.

SEVEN

RAILROAD CAMP

A careful inspection of the storage facility for railroad supplies here in Durango yesterday afternoon hadn't told me much. Matthew, the nervous clerk, had let me in and hurried back to the shack where he kept the records.

I stopped Matthew before he slipped away. "Matthew, I heard there is a marshal who is pretty much the law around here. Does he keep an office in town?"

Matthew nodded and shook his head all at once, looking even more uncomfortable than usual. "Sometimes he does some work in the jail over there." He jerked his head sideways and to his left. I had already seen the jail, so I nodded.

"He's got the western slopes, over to the western border of the state and on over to Silverton on the east, right?" I asked.

Matthew's head bobbed up and down and he tried

to make his escape one more time. "And, Matthew," I said slowly, "did you talk to Cleo Ward yesterday?"

He nodded his head miserably. "I did."

"Okay," I said. "I may not need to make a fake report of shipment of valuable supplies and materials."

He brightened right up.

"But, if I do," I continued, "I'll be back in town to let you know personally, and it's real important," I said, dragging out the words, "that you don't tell anybody—not ever. We're clear on that, right?"

He dragged his toe in the dirt and mumbled something.

"Couldn't really hear you, Matthew. Need to hear you."

"We're clear," he said, making eye contact for the first time. He turned and hurried away. I could see I was making that boy's life miserable.

He was out the door before I remembered something else I needed from Matthew. He looked up and watched me as I came back to the desk. "Something else," I said. "What's getting stolen, mostly? Tools, spikes, nails, that kind of thing? Or the big, heavy stuff? Iron girders and heavy beams of timber?"

His head bobbed another time or two. "Little stuff, mostly. Spikes, hammers, saws, nails. A few of the smaller iron pieces and some boards."

I retraced my steps outside. That was pretty much what I'd expected. I didn't know how they could take that heavy stuff anywhere unless they took it somewhere on the train. Why rob a train to put the stuff back on the train?

Returning to the warehouse, I took a tour around the outside, looking for any place somebody had forced their way in. Finding nothing, I went on inside to have a look. There was a little daylight coming in from a small window at the top on both sides. It was dim and dusty, for starters, and stuff seemed to be scattered everywhere.

I moved around the shelves, seeing nothing that looked all that valuable. I wondered if Matthew had records for what was supposed to be in here. Moving on to some crates and barrels in the corners, I could see they all had labels. Mostly, they were marked as spikes and nails. I tilted a couple to satisfy myself they were full.

There were a couple of locked cabinets. I tested the locks—they were secure. I made a note to ask Matthew what was in the cabinets. Then I made a lap around the inside, looking again for any place somebody could have let themselves in with a crowbar. I saw nothing to suggest anybody had forced their way in.

I locked it up behind me and stood outside the storage, staring across the tracks. There were more rail tracks over there, running north, it looked like. I'd heard there was another outfit running a train up to Denver. I would have to remember to ask about that.

Now it was time to look for the marshal. I hadn't figured there were break-ins happening in town. Now I was sure whatever robberies the railroad was dealing with were happening on the rails between here and the camp. There were too many workers who could see it out there at the camp.

There were two men in the jail office when I pushed through the doors. There was a smaller man, younger than I'd have thought, maybe about my age. A much bigger, older man was lounging against the wall near the door when I came in.

The smaller man stood and moved over to meet me. "Marshal Bert Anderson," he greeted me. His eyes took me in with a friendly but curious look. "I'm the marshal around here, and parts east and west," he explained.

"Latigo Smith," I began. The marshal interrupted me. "Right, Deacon left me a note about you! Gonna help with railroad security around here. Glad to have the help." He pointed to the guy who had moved away from the wall behind me. "Brett Wallace, my deputy."

Wallace shook my hand without ever looking me in the eye. His grip was powerful, and when I glanced down, I saw some scarred hands. This guy had been in more than his share of knuckle-and-skull fights. He mumbled something about making some rounds and left.

I took a seat. Anderson explained his schedule to me and jotted down some notes on how I could reach him by telegram if I needed to. He wrote the place where he stayed while in town and told me he was glad to help. My worries about a crooked marshal disappeared. I was wondering about that deputy, though.

"Tell me," I said, "how did you wind up being the marshal in these parts?"

He looked a little embarrassed. "John Routt, our first governor, he knew me when I was a kid. Friend of the family. I took a turn in the army, and when I came out, he said he needed the help." He pointed out the door. "Wallace, out there, knows all the folks around here and came on as my deputy."

I chewed the fat with him for another twenty minutes, then took off. I felt good about the marshal, except he seemed pretty green. I was about the same age, but I'd been around hard times a lot more, I was pretty sure. I wondered where he had served in the army.

The deputy, Wallace, was a different story. Probably pushing forty, he was the old bull of the woods around here, I was betting. I didn't feel nearly as good about him.

I checked the watch in my pocket and squinted over at the railroad stop on the edge of town. I figured I had just about enough time to see Joanna at the bakery for a few minutes. I would grab my knapsack and what-not from the boarding house and head up the tracks to check in with Holt and the crew up there.

———

I sat at the edge of a car. The door was open, and I was the only one on the train besides the engineer, near as I could tell. My legs were out the door and I was swinging my feet over the tracks as we rumbled down the line toward the camp. I thought passenger cars were a rough ride, the time or two I'd taken the train, but this here cargo car was enough to rattle my teeth out of my head. The railroad didn't much like making these runs, they had to have an engine on the back to go back to town. They used a handcart when they could. There were a few supplies in these cars—too many for the handcart.

When the railroad camp steamed into view around the corner, I was mighty glad to see it. I hopped down before it had completely stopped moving, then moved back two cars to unload my horse. From the look in his eye, I don't think he liked that trip any more than me. I tipped my cap to the engineer and went on a brief tour of the camp. Men behind me unloaded some supplies from the train.

Men were lining up for lunch. I could smell charred meat, so I knew Holt must be doing his job. He was probably out hunting now. I passed up the food offered by a guy named Cookie and rode around the outskirts of the camp. There were several small tents set up, usually in a circle around the sites of small campfires. The railroad hadn't built any temporary shelters for the workers.

I rode in a half circle around the edge of the camp. Seeing a little stockade of some kind, I rode closer. I could hear the neighing of horses. Had to be the temporary corral they would need, I figured. I dismounted and found the makeshift gate. I pushed in and walked around. There was a crude shelter in the corner. Somebody had grabbed some boards and made themselves a little lean-to. Probably just shelter for the guard when it rained.

I walked in a little closer and saw something else. Cigarette butts. Lots of them. I kneeled down to take a look, then walked a little circle around the opening of the hut. There were a lot of bootprints. I kneeled down and thought about it. One man on guard at night wouldn't leave this many bootprints or cigarette butts. This was a meeting place of some kind.

Now I knew where to make my camp. There wouldn't be any robberies tonight or in the early hours of the morning, because there was no train coming with fresh materials. Not tonight, but I could arrange that big shipment of materials. At least I could make them think there was a train coming in the next couple of days.

I unsaddled my horse and turned him out in the corral, then carried my gear out and climbed a little rise near the corral. I laid out my bedroll in a thick stand of junipers and looked down on the corral. I had a feeling I might have found the staging area for robberies of incoming trains. At the least, it looked like a meeting place for some folks ready to go out and do stuff they didn't want anybody else to know about.

＿＿

After I had set up my own little camp and looked around some more, inspecting the tracks north of here, I rode on out to Red Mountain Pass. The rails snaked up the mountainside. I couldn't really tell what was holding 'em up there.

Deacon spotted me as soon as I rode up. He slapped me on the back a few times and took me on a brief tour. He began by taking me to the base of the pass and pointing up.

"We had to clear the trees and underbrush on both sides," he hollered. "That took us a few weeks. Now you can see we're laying in beams and piers for support."

The sound of hammers and saws was enough to leave my ears ringing after just a couple of minutes. It didn't take long to see the railroad had spent a lot of money on those iron beams and huge timbers. There were plenty of tools and supplies up there, too. I wondered for the first time how they were getting stuff hauled away for sale after the robberies.

Deacon interrupted my thinking with a slap on the back. "This here's Buck," he boomed. I turned around to see a tall, bald man with a flat nose. He was big, too. My ma would have said *he has muscles on his muscles*.

Buck took my hand like he was gonna squash it, but I gave as good as I took. Deacon looked a little surprised when Buck dropped my hand and backed away. "Buck, here, can help ya keep these guys in line," Deacon said. They walked away.

I watched them leave, wondering why Deacon had said he needed somebody to *bust some heads* when he had Buck. I had a feeling I was being set up for something. When they were gone, I went back to wondering what was happening with all the stolen tools and supplies. Where did they go, and how did they get there?

Holt trailed into camp in the late afternoon. He had two deer—a buck laid over the saddle in front of him and a doe roped over a pack horse he led in behind him. He pulled up, looked over the crowd, and spotted me helping Cookie lift a barrel of beans out of a wagon.

"Could use a little help cleanin' these deer, Pard!" he said, sliding down out the saddle. Nobody else moved a muscle. I grabbed a knife and went over to help as he lifted the carcasses off the saddles. I could feel Deacon's eyes following me. We moved out of earshot and kneeled to skin the animals.

"Learn anything interestin' in town, Lat?" Holt glanced over his shoulder as he spoke. He noticed Deacon at the edge of the campfire Cookie was building, but Deacon didn't come any closer.

"Yeah, more than I bargained on," I muttered as I stripped away the skin from a foreleg. "They're losin' a lot of stuff—smaller, easier to carry stuff. I think it's taken off the trains between here and Silverton. The engineer must be in on it, otherwise we'd hear more fuss about it when he gets to camp or when he gets back to town. Mebbe other folks from the railroad are part of this."

Holt nodded, keeping his back to Deacon. "I heard a conversation the other day when I was down in my deer shelter. One of 'em talkin' was Deacon. The other 'un I couldn't see, but it sounded like his name is Wallace. Wallace was asking Deacon how come he hired you. Didn't sound none too happy about it."

I stared at him. "Wallace," I mumbled.

"What? Do you know somebody named Wallace?"

"Met him yesterday, back in town. Didn't like him much, neither. Gets worse, though. He's the deputy marshal for this southwestern part of Colorado."

"Dang." Holt let out a low whistle, then glanced over his shoulder again. Deacon seemed to have lost interest in them. For now, anyway, he thought. "Whaddya wanna do, Pard?"

I let my thoughts chase each other around in my noggin for a while. Finally, I told Holt what I was planning. "We've got a couple things on our side," I told him. "First off, Deacon's boss was in town an' I met him this morning. I think maybe he suspects Deacon a little. Told me I could report to him direct if I want to. Also met the marshal, along with that Wallace guy. The marshal's a little green, but I don't think he's crooked."

I shot a glance back over my shoulder. Deacon was walking away with that bruiser named Buck. I didn't much like the thought of having a dustup with old Buck there, but I had a feeling I would have to.

I went back to cleaning the doe. "Here's what I wanna do. Tomorrow, I'll ride out with you like I'm going huntin' with you. I'll slip away, ride back to town, and tell the clerk to send a note out to Deacon, telling him there's a big shipment of stuff coming out here two nights from tonight. That clerk will have a messenger boy ride out or something. He'll get word to Deacon."

Holt nodded. "Shipment comin', okay."

"Not really," I murmured.

"Huh?" Holt's forehead was all twisted up.

"It's a trap," I explained. "I'll let Deacon think

there's a big shipment coming he can rob. If he's crooked, like we think, he and his boys will wait to rob it. I'm gonna mess up their plans. You and me."

Holt moaned. "Thanks, Pard. Lucky for me, I packed a double-barreled shotgun in my gear. I'm gonna have Ole Betsy ready to go."

"You might need it," I agreed.

━━━

Joanna washed off the tabletops after the morning rush. First thing to do, she decided, was to find an old-timer with some stories about trapping, mining, and the route to Los Angeles in the old days. She had no intention of giving her grandfather's real name, though. The last thing she needed was to touch off another search for Barnabus Smith's black pebbles.

Deciding she would have to trust somebody, Joanna elected to ask Ma if she knew anybody who'd been around and done those things.

Ma paused over a bowl of dough, her arms covered in flour up to the elbows. "Well," she said doubtfully. "There's old Hank Brown. He done some of that stuff. Comes in here with his daughter about once a week. Sometimes he remembers stuff he don't really remember, though." She pointed at her forehead. "A little bit tetched, ya know? I'll tell you when they come in next time."

Joanna had to wait only a day. She was pulling loaves of bread from the brick fireplace when Ma tapped her on the shoulder and pointed. "Hank Brown," she explained. "The woman with him is his daughter, Emma. Don't let him tie you up in knots," she cautioned. "He'll keep talkin' until you're ready to walk away."

Joanna carried their order to the table and gave refills on their coffee. She set the coffeepot down and turned back to the table. "I think you might have known my grandpa," she said to Hank Brown.

"Huh?" Brown had put his hand up to his ear to act as a speaking trumpet. "What did ya say, young lady?" he bellowed.

Emma leaned over to speak in his ear. "She says you might have known her grandfather." Emma pointed at an empty chair. "Join us, please."

Brown squinted at her doubtfully. "Grandpa, huh? Well, maybe. What was his name?"

"James Maker," Joanna blurted. It was as good a name as any. She would just have to remember later what she'd told them. "My grandpa, James, used to do some trapping and mining, things like that. Up near Ouray."

Hank Brown stared at the wall. He stopped to slurp his coffee. "James Maker," he repeated. He shook his head slowly. "Don't remember no James Maker."

Joanna pretended to be disappointed.

"Too bad," she said. "I was thinking about going up there to see where he lived and did his trapping and all." She got up to refill his coffee.

"Maybe you just forgot, Dad," Emma prompted. "Tell her what you know about the trapping and mining up there, back when you did those things."

"Hmm, well, trappin' was pretty good back then. Beaver, mostly. There was some good sharp twists and forks and underbrush at the edge of the Ouray River, out east of the old fort. Good for beaver. Pelts brought us a good price, back in those days."

"Do any panning?" Joanna asked.

"HUH? Shore we did." Hank took his volume down a peg or two. "Did some pannin' out west of the fort, on the Ouray River. Fort's gone, you know? Gone now." He stared at the wall, mumbling to himself.

This was better than she'd hoped for. Joanna decided on one last question. "Where did you sell the beaver pelts," she asked. "Was Denver around back then?"

Hank snorted. "Cherry Creek? Nah, twasn't nuthin' there. You wanted a good price, you had to take 'em to Los Angeles. Had to foller the river west quite a while, then hold 'er south for Durango. Had to avoid the big peaks and the Injuns...I remember one time, them Utes come after us..."

Ma approached the table. "Joanna, can you help me in the back?"

Joanna stood and followed Ma. "Thanks," she said under her breath. "Thought you might need a rescue, dear," Ma explained.

EIGHT
SETTING THE TRAP

I was up at sunrise. My horse was picketed a short distance away. I'd taken him out of the makeshift corral after dinner last night. Getting away this morning was maybe the most important part, and I didn't want anybody holding me up at the corral. The crew was used to Holt being gone at sunup, and I needed to get away with him. Some of the best hunting was when the deer and elk came to water at first light.

If a few guys saw me leave with Holt, that was good. We'd let it be known last night I would help with the hunting today. Deacon had shrugged and said nothing when I told him. Just as long as I stayed out of his hair, he was probably happy, I figured.

The sun was peeking over the mountain tops in front of us as we rode east out of camp. This was the direction Holt had been taking every morning so far. As long as he came back with meat, everybody was happy, no matter which way he went.

We reached the stream where Holt had settled down every morning to watch for game. He pointed to the southwest. "I have scouted that way a little. You can ride alongside the railroad tracks after you get a mile or two south and west from here, then cut south and west. When you reach the railroad tracks, you can follow them west into town. If anybody comes along, you can get into cover in the trees pretty fast. I'll wait for you here so we can ride back together this afternoon."

I nodded and caught up the reins to my horse.

"Hold on."

Holt came over and slipped out of his jacket. "Gimme yours," he said. "The crew mostly recognize this coat as mine, I expect. I've worn it every morning since I've been here."

I saw what he was doing. If anybody saw me from the back, they would think I was Holt. We switched hats while we were at it. I settled the hat on my head and put the coat on. The sleeves stopped about four inches short of my wrists.

Holt snorted. "Serves you right for bein' too tall. Jest make sure that pretty girl at the bakery don't see you ridin' in looking like a scarecrow."

I grinned and turned my horse west by southwest. I gave the camp a wide berth, skirting around it until I guessed I was at least a mile west of it. After that, I took off Holt's coat, rolled it up, and stuffed it in my saddlebag. He was right. I looked like a scarecrow in that thing.

A thought struck me on the way into town. I had been puzzling over where they could take all this heavy stuff they were stealing. Iron beams, caskets of nails, things like that were too heavy to carry on a packhorse. Even saws and hammers would weigh a lot if you stole enough to matter. I had a feeling if I could solve that riddle, I would know what they were up to.

I moved over to within fifty yards of the track and cut back and forth as I worked my way into town. By the time I got there, I was just as puzzled as ever. Durango was awake and busy by the time I rode down Main Street. I wasted no time getting to the railroad office. I pushed through the door without knocking. I knew Deacon was still back there at the camp.

It surprised me to find Cleo Ward in there with Matthew. They were looking at some papers when I walked in. Ward had a frown on his face. "We've lost a lot," he muttered to Matthew.

Ward straightened up when he saw me and walked over. "Give me some good news, Lat," he said hopefully.

"Well, I been doing a lot of thinkin', coming into town," I told him. I looked over at Matthew. "First off, I want you to get word to Deacon there's a shipment coming in with lots of supplies. This stuff comes in from Denver, right?"

"Right." It was Ward who jumped in with that answer. "We have to bring it in on Denver & Rio Grande Western, our competitor. Costs us a fortune, but we gotta pay it. Only way to bring that stuff in. Stagecoaches and pack horses can't carry it."

Suddenly, I had an idea of what was happening. It was when he said their stuff was coming in from

Denver on a competitor that I thought of it. I didn't want to let Matthew in on it, mainly 'cause he just didn't need to know. I stared at Ward.

"What?" he barked. "You still wanna set up a trap?"

"Yep." I looked back at Matthew. "You send a note, set up the papers, whatever you have to do, get word out to Deacon there's a big shipment coming in, two nights from tonight. Lots of tools, the kind of stuff that's gettin' stolen. Let me see it before you send off the messenger."

I put a hand on Ward's shoulder. "Can you step outside with me?"

We stepped out to the porch. I kept looking across those tracks.

"Out with it," Ward boomed. "You're on to something. Who's been stealing our stuff?"

I raised a hand in the air. "I've just got to ask a couple questions first." Ward nodded impatiently. "Your goods come in from Denver on the other railroad. How do they get on your train? What happens after that?"

Ward smoothed down his hair and calmed himself down a little. "When we know it's here, Deacon brings some of his boys back from camp, and they shift the stuff to our line, one of our cars. Deacon has a couple boys ride shotgun with it back to camp. Never reported a robbery, not the boys riding guard nor the engineer. They're all in on it, right, the engineer and Deacon's boys? They must be."

"Mebbe not the engineer," I told him. I knew this

next part would be tough. "How long you known Deacon?" I asked.

Ward stared at me. "Ten years. Rode with him in the calvary during the war. Best man at my wedding. What are you saying, Smith?" His eyes were shootin' bullets at me.

I heaved a sigh. "I think Deacon is behind it. Most of it, anyway. Probably got him a crooked partner over at Denver & Rio Grande Western. Your stuff comes in, Deacon and his boys move some of it to your car. The rest they sell back to Denver & Rio Grande Western an' it goes back to Denver. They use it up there to build some more rail lines."

I looked over at Ward. He was still mad, but I could see it made sense to him, too. "The engineer never reports it got robbed because nuthin' happens on the way to your camp. It was never in your car." I started to say more, but I'd run out of words. I shut up and let Ward percolate on what I'd said.

Ward stared at his boots and said nothing for a long time. Finally, he raised his head to look at me. He knew I was right. I could see it in his eyes. It made too much sense.

"So," he said in a low rumble, "you sent out the message to lure Deacon in here with his boys. What happens next?"

"We're waiting for them," I said. "We catch 'em stealing the stuff. Rest of it is up to you." I turned back. "One more thing, we need Marshal Anderson here. With a little luck, we'll catch the guy or the people with the other railroad who are in on this." I stopped, then added one more thought. "Just

Marshall Anderson. Tell him not to bring his deputy."

Ward heaved another sigh. "Wallace," he said. "Is he crooked too?"

"Not sure," I said. "Not sure." I walked off down the street. I wanted to stop into the bakery and see Joanna, but it didn't seem like a good time to do it. I still had a lot to think about. Thing is, I'd not had any breakfast, and it was close to noon. My stomach was rubbin' against my backbone. I couldn't forget that breakfast I'd had at the bakery the other day. That made up my mind for me. I headed for Ma's Bakery.

One thing still bothered me. What was going on at that lean-to at the makeshift corral back at camp? I turned that one over in my brain a few times. Maybe I'd made too much of that. Maybe Deacon's boys just met up there before they came to town to meet the train.

═══

The smell of fresh-brewed coffee was the first thing Miller smelled when he walked into the café. Wallace was right behind him. They picked their usual table overlooking the street outside. Miller surveyed the room and saw nothing unusual. He could hear the usual hum of voices and the clinking of glasses back in the kitchen. He relaxed and waited for a report from Wallace. He was expecting another good one. This railroad thing was just about the sweetest setup he'd ever run.

Wallace held out his coffee cup and watched the

girl as she filled his cup and walked back to the kitchen. He avoided looking at Miller, which was Miller's first tipoff. The news wasn't as good as he was expecting this morning.

"What?" Miller hissed. "Somethin' going on I don't know about?"

Wallace looked around. Nobody could possibly hear them talking. He shook his head, then shrugged, then grabbed his coffee cup before looking at Miller. Wallace considered himself a scary guy, but he knew he wasn't like Miller. Didn't want to be like Miller. Finally, he looked Miller in the eye.

"Ain't nuthin' bad happened," Wallace mumbled. The boys are layin' track, up that Red Mountain Pass and we're just waitin' for the next shipment. We'll come back to town and take care of it like always."

Miller leaned in. "What's got you so skittish, then?" he demanded. "You ain't looked me in the eye twice since we come in here. You scairt to be seen around me now?"

Wallace shook his head. "Nobody in this town knows you're anything but the guy that owns The Rusty Bucket. It ain't that. Deacon had to hire a guy to look into the stuff that we been stealin' from the railroad. Hired him several days ago. He's been out with the crew. Him an' some other guy that got hired to hunt meat for the crew."

Miller thumped his coffee cup back down on the table and sucked in his breath. "Deacon done that? What'd he do a fool thing like that for?"

Heads turned in their direction. Miller forced

himself to relax and lean back in his chair. "What'd he do that for?" he repeated in a quieter voice.

Wallace waited while the girl refilled his coffee. "Ward made him do it."

Miller stared daggers across the table. "Who's Ward? Have Deacon tell him to mind his own business!"

Wallace shook his head, waiting for Miller to cool off. "Ward is Deacon's boss. He runs the railroad in this part of the country. If Deacon gets hisself fired, we won't see no more of that railroad money," he reminded Miller. "We got to have Deacon to make this work."

"Mebbe somethin' needs to happen to this Ward guy," Miller said quietly.

Wallace gulped some coffee. This was what he'd been afraid of. He leaned in. "If somethin' happens to Ward, the railroad guards will be all over this place," Wallace hissed. "And then the railroad will send in somebody else. They'll get the marshal an' maybe even the guvnor involved. No end of trouble."

Miller turned several shades of red. He wasn't used to anybody talking to him like this. Wallace waited it out while Miller cooled.

"Who are the guards you're talkin' about?" Miller grumbled. "Where are they?" Wallace shrugged. "You'll see 'em if you push hard enough. Some pretty salty gunhands, some of 'em."

"Okay, let's hear what you got planned," Miller mumbled.

Wallace took his time. He'd been thinking about this. He was just a shadow out at the railroad camp.

Only Deacon knew he was out there, watching from the shadows. He wanted to keep it that way.

"First of all, I don't think this guy has seen anything out there. You know the robberies don't happen at the camp, anyway. Let him nose around. Deacon's worried about it, but what's he gonna find out there?"

Miller got quiet, looking out the window and watching the street. Wallace knew Miller was most dangerous when he got quiet.

"Who is this guy that Deacon hired?" Miller hissed. "What's his name? What's he like? I wanna discourage him from looking into things."

Wallace folded his hands on the table. "Name's Latigo Smith. He come up from Texas somewhere. Used to be a deppity sheriff. My guess is he's got some bark on him and we don't wanna mess with him if we don't have to. We ain't done nuthin' to make him suspicious yet."

Miller bored in on him. "I want him discouraged from pokin' around things. Tell me how you're gonna make that happen. This here is on you. I need Deacon to make the railroad arrangements, but this here is yore job."

Wallace smoothed his mustache and stared at the table. "Buck. Maybe Buck can do it. Bust him up a little, I mean. This Smith guy might be good with his guns. Dunno about his fists. I can tell Deacon to set Buck on him."

Miller relaxed for the first time since they'd come in. He waved at the waitress to bring him his usual breakfast. "Good," he muttered. "Tell Buck to bust him up enough that he might just want to go back to Texas." He mumbled a few more things to himself, then looked back at Wallace. "What's this guy look like? We seen him in town?"

"I have," Wallace answered. "Met him with the marshal. He's tall, big guy…" Wallace stopped and stared out the window. "He looks like that guy, walkin' by outside." He stared again. "That's him," he told Miller. "That's Latigo Smith, right there."

I came back just the way I'd left this morning, using the railroad tracks to guide me right back to the camp. I found Holt loading a cut-up elk carcass on the pack-horse. I whistled to let him know I was coming in, then helped him finish the loading.

When we had finished loading the elk on the pack-horse, I caught Holt up on my talk with Ward back in town. "They're stealin' stuff right there in the train yard," I finished up. "I'm pretty sure of it. Some of it goes from one railroad car to another, an' the rest steams right back up to Denver."

Holt whistled softly and thought it over. "So, there's gonna be a little dustup down at the train yard in a couple nights?" He grinned for a second. "I still got my shotgun, Old Betsy," he offered. "I'd be happy to tag along."

"Glad for the help." I nodded.

Holt walked over to a tree and cut a couple switches off with his knife, then went and pulled some string and a couple of hooks from his saddlebag. He pulled a small shovel off the packhorse, walked down, and started digging down near the stream where the elk had come for water.

"What're you doing now?" I asked.

Holt reached down and pulled some worms out of the dirt he'd just dug up. He hooked the worms and tied the hooks to the string and the switches he'd cut from the trees. I walked past him and stared down at the brown trout swimming past in the mountain stream.

"You an' me, I figger we could take a break from eatin' deer meat and elk every night," Holt grinned.

I grabbed one of the switches. "Good idea," I told him.

Wallace sat in the shade of a stand of junipers, his usual meeting spot with Deacon. He couldn't be seen at the railroad camp. His cover as a deputy marshal was too good to lose. He swore under his breath. He'd followed Latigo Smith out of Durango, but Smith was a little too trail-wise and canny. Wallace had lost the trail somewhere along the way back from town. Still, he had a message to pass on to Deacon.

Deacon arrived on time. Wallace passed on how Smith had doubled back into town this morning instead of hunting with Holt. He relayed Miller's orders about turning Buck loose on Smith to stop the *snooping around* Smith was doing.

Deacon was stunned at the news, his jaw dropped open. "What's he know?" Deacon demanded. "I got a message from the clerk this mornin'—there's a big shipment coming in. Smith know about that?"

Wallace struck a match and cupped it with his hand to light a cigar. He shook his head. "Nah, he don't know what we're doing at the train yard. Just tell Buck to go settle his hash. That'll be the end of it. You can tell Ward you done your job, an' Smith jest up and quit."

A grin spread slowly across Deacon's face. "Yeah, Buck don't like him much. That's a fact. Okay, I'll have Buck do it tomorrow after I've gone back to town. I can tell Ward I wasn't there to stop the fight."

The trout was almost as good as I thought it would be. I hadn't had any fresh-caught trout since I was a kid. I leaned back against my saddle while Holt put out the campfire. A figure moved toward us in the fading light. When he got closer, I could see it was Deacon. I stood and watched him come in.

"Just wanted to let you boys know I'm goin' back to Durango for a couple days," Deacon told us. He looked at me. "You're gonna be in charge around here. I told Buck. Just tell him what you want done."

I nodded and watched him walk away. "Holt," I said over my shoulder. "I'm bein' set up for something tomorrow. Promise me you'll keep it a fair fight."

NINE
MILLER

C ookie rang his dinner triangle at six in the morning, just like he always did. Today was the day Deacon had left me in charge. Holt and I both did something a little different—we lined up with the other workers for Cookie's bacon, biscuits, and coffee. Deacon told the crew before he left I was in charge today and tomorrow. We got some stares when we lined up.

Buck walked along the breakfast line and stopped in front of Holt. "How come you ain't out there huntin' already?" Buck challenged. "You ain't never been in the breakfast line."

"Just decided when I woke up," Holt answered, returning his stare. "I heard Cookie's biscuits was the best in this-here state."

That brought some laughs from up and down the line. Cookie glared at everybody. That dried up the laughs. Didn't nobody want to be on Cookie's bad side. A man could go hungry that way. Buck didn't seem to think it was funny, either.

Buck jerked a thumb in the direction Holt usually took when he rode out of camp. "Git out there and start huntin'," he ordered.

Holt didn't move and traded stares with Buck. "He'll stay for breakfast if he wants to," I announced.

Buck backed off a step. There was a buzz of chatter from the line. He stared at the Colt in my gun belt. "You've got that shootin' iron on yore hip," he muttered.

"That's right, I do," I barked. "I'll be giving the orders for the day right after breakfast. You'll get your orders then."

The crew shot looks back and forth from me to Buck. He glared but backed away. Holt moved up beside me. "He's gonna challenge you to a fistfight, you know that, right? He don't want to mess with that Colt."

"Yeah, he will," I agreed. "Probably right after breakfast when I give the orders." I looked over to see Buck in a little huddle with two of his henchmen. I nodded in that direction. "He's setting things up for a fight," I murmured. "You make sure to have Ole Betsy handy after breakfast. I'll give him his fight then."

Holt let out a low whistle. "You're gonna fight him knuckle-and-skull? He's built like a Brahma bull. You sure you wanna do this?"

"I am." I took a step or two forward in the line. "I'm gonna have some breakfast first, though. He'll probly leave a welt or two on me, but he'll lose a tooth or two and his breakfast, mebbe in that order. Just don't let those buddies of his work me over if I get close to 'em during the fight."

Holt grinned. "Okay, pard." He looked over at the two men talking to Buck and staring over their shoulders at us. "I think I'll stand behind those two with Old Betsy. That oughta keep their hands in their pockets."

We finished up with breakfast, and the crew was quiet. I got up and walked to stand in front of the breakfast campfire, which I'd noticed was where Deacon always went to give his morning orders. Buck got up and walked over, standing a few feet away and staring at me. I ignored him.

"All right, everybody, listen up!" I announced. "You've got two regular teams, right? One team measures and marks the spots for rail ties, the other team lays 'em down?"

A few heads nodded.

"Okay," I went on, "switch off from yesterday. The team that measured yesterday lays ties today. The team that laid ties yesterday measures today. Everybody got it? We're aimin' for five hundred yards of ties by supper time!"

"Other way around!" Buck barked. "Keep the jobs you had yesterday!" He grinned at me. "You've still got that smokewagon on yore hip. You salty enough to give the orders without it?"

A small circle started to form around us. I saw Holt slip away toward our campsite from last night. I had to give him time to get the shotgun and get back.

"You ever been in a real fight, Buck?" I asked. "Or do you just get your buddies over there to throw a man on the ground while you put your boots to him?" I unhooked the buckle on my gun belt.

I saw the red flush start up his neck from my insult, but then he grinned when I handed my gun belt to Cookie. He clenched his fists a couple times. "Yore about to get a proper lesson, Mr. High-and-Mighty." He backed away a few steps and pointed at the breakfast fire. "I'd hate to throw you in that fire right off. I'm gonna have some fun with you first."

From the corner of my eye, I saw Holt move in behind Buck's two enforcers. The sound of both barrels cocking wasn't lost on anybody. "Fair fight, boys," Holt said. Buck's enforcers slid a few steps to the side. Holt stayed with them, and they stopped moving. One barrel apiece wasn't good odds for anybody.

I was ready now. I moved away from the campfire and circled Buck a couple times. I had a good six inches of reach on him, and I planned to use it.

Buck charged and swung a wild right hook at my head. I leaned back to avoid it, then stepped in and gave him a sharp, jolting punch to his left eye. His head snapped back. He shook his head to clear his brain, then swung a wild roundhouse left that I easily sidestepped.

We circled warily, then he charged again and swung a right uppercut at my head. I stepped inside the punch and ducked, then lifted my left fist and sunk it into his belly up to my wrist. I heard the air whoosh out of him. He bent over and put his hands on his knees, sucking wind.

"Don't feel too good right after breakfast, huh?" I grinned and sent a hard straight overhand right into his mouth when he straightened up.

He cursed and charged again, swinging that big overhand right. I stayed outside his reach and delivered another hard jab to his left eye. It was swelling shut. He shook his head like an angry bear, let out a howl, and charged.

I met him halfway with another straight right to his mouth. He spun away, blood starting from his mouth. He leaned over and spat out a tooth.

I continued to circle. He was still dangerous, but I knew I could finish him before long. Those jabs had swelled his left eye almost shut, so I knew he couldn't see from that side. His chest was heaving, and I was pretty sure his breakfast wouldn't stay down much longer.

He charged again, trying to get his arms around me to take me to the ground. I knew he'd be dangerous if he could wrap me up. I stepped aside, stuck out my foot to trip him, and shoved the back of his head on the way down. He landed hard in the dust and lay there, sucking wind.

He got up and circled, not sure what to do now. He lifted that big right hand like he was going for my head, then stopped and hooked with his left. It was a good move, and it almost got me. The left hand landed a hard blow to my ribs. This guy could punch.

We circled again, and I faked an overhand right to

his left eye. He winced and pulled back, dropping his guard. I followed with a straight left that smashed his nose. He bent over and grabbed his knees, glaring at me with that one good eye.

When he roared and charged me again, I stepped in and lifted a left hook to his chin. I heard his teeth snap together, and he went down hard again.

I stood over him. "Be smart and stay down this time," I told him.

He did the first smart thing he'd done today and stayed down like I told him. I looked around at the crew. They were staring at Buck, down there in the dust, like they couldn't believe what they'd seen. It was a new sight for them.

"You've all got your jobs for today," I barked. "We need five hundred yards of track! Get to it!" They scattered, grabbed some tools, and loaded up to move out and start the day.

Buck had come to his knees, struggling to get up. He fished around inside his mouth with a finger, then touched his nose, which was pouring blood. I handed him a rag and told him to hold it against his nose and mouth to stop the bleeding. "Take a couple hours before you go to work if you need to," I said.

I turned to walk away. "Hey," he said, struggling to his feet. "You beat me fair and square." He turned and stumbled away.

━━

Deacon met Miller and Wallace in the usual spot—the back room of The Rusty Bucket. He was whistling on his way through the door, prompting a glare from Miller. Deacon had always suspected that Miller helped himself to a little too much of his own whiskey some nights. The next morning, he would always be in a foul mood. Today, Miller was like a mama bear without her cubs. Deacon stopped whistling and sat down at the table.

"Well?" Miller growled.

Deacon looked at Miller blankly, then looked at Wallace, who shrugged. "Uh, I left at first light," Deacon said. "I can tell Ward I wasn't there to stop the fight. Buck and his boys will work Smith over real good. He'll probly just pull his freight afterward. I can tell Ward he didn't find nuthin' while he was here."

Miller nodded, then grabbed at his head and cursed under his breath. "And the shipment tomorrow night? You ready for that?"

Deacon nodded confidently. "I have my usual crew of four men. They'll leave after dark tomorrow night and git here to move the stuff. They can foller the tracks into town, so no problem finding us in the dark. I'll pay 'em the usual and give 'em a day off like always. They'll spend most of it in yore saloon out front."

Miller grunted and shifted in his chair. "What else do we know about this Latigo Smith?" he demanded. This time, he looked at Wallace. "You foller him around in town like I told ya last time?"

Wallace nodded. A thin, cruel smile crossed his lips. "He went down to Ma's Bakery and stayed in there a while. He was talkin' to a purty, new girl working in there. Never saw her before. I think maybe he's sweet on the new girl. Want me to see what else I kin find out?"

Miller shook his head, then winced at the pain that shot between his temples. He stood and moaned, then moved over to the coffeepot. He poured himself a cup, then moved back to the table. Deacon just watched. He'd never thought coffee helped him the times when he'd been in Miller's shape, but he knew better than to talk.

Miller gulped some coffee. "Nope, you get back out to the railroad camp and tell me what happened after Buck took care of this Smith guy. Let me know if Smith is still around. And his friend, the hunter. Send him packing too if he ain't gone yet. You," he said, pointing at Deacon, "get ready for the shipment tomorrow night. I'll go and see about this new girl at Ma's Bakery."

Miller quit talking, and the other two knew they'd been dismissed. He was still staring into his coffee cup when they filed out of the room.

⊏⊐

Joanna had found an old, hand-drawn map of western Colorado at the general store. She'd paid twenty-five cents for it. The shopkeeper's wife had shaken her head at her husband. It was clear she thought Joanna was getting swindled. Joanna made her escape from the general store before the husband and wife started arguing about it.

She had gone over that map in her room at the boarding house until she had just about memorized it.

The more she looked at it, the less sense it made to her that somebody had found gold in the Ouray River and tried to take it to Los Angeles to cash it in.

Denver and Leadville didn't really exist in 1840, she knew that, but there were some mining settlements around that were a lot closer than California. Why wouldn't somebody have taken it there, rather than through Durango, probably on their way to Los Angeles?

Joanna thought it was more likely that whoever had first found those black pebbles had been somebody like her grandfather. Somebody who was a fur trader taking pelts to Los Angeles. That was a big fur trading center in those days, she knew that. It wasn't her grandfather or Pegleg Smith who had panned that gold, though. The letter said Ezekiel had seen black pebbles before, but it didn't sound like he'd done anything with them. Pegleg's letter made it clear he'd just found the nuggets on the mesa. Those had belonged to somebody else.

Maybe if an original fur trader had stopped to pan a river near Durango, he could have run from the Utes and left the gold on a mesa top, just like Pegleg and Ezekiel did later. That's assuming Lat was right, and somebody had mined the black pebbles in a river and left them on top of the mesa, not knowing they were gold.

Whoever they were, Joanna reasoned, they either decided the *pebbles* weren't worth anything, just as Ezekiel had, or they'd had to clear out in a hurry, leaving them behind.

Joanna sighed and put away the map. Maybe she

would try to talk to Hank Brown again at the coffee shop. Hopefully, she could keep him on track with the conversation this time. She looked again at the map and traced a river with her finger, then bent to read the name. "Animas River," she murmured to herself. Just north of Durango. Maybe she would talk to Hank about that.

———

It was two days later before Hank came back to the bakery with his daughter Emma. When Joanna brought the coffee, Hank's eyes lit up. Emma shook a warning finger at him when Joanna arrived with their order.

"No wearing her out with old stories about trapping and mining in the old days," she scolded him.

"I don't mind," Joanna said, taking a seat. "It reminds me a little of talking to my grandfather."

"Yeah, them Utes was comin' at us one mornin'…" Hank started, then glanced guiltily at his daughter.

"Eat, Dad," Emma moaned. She shoved a pastry onto his plate.

Hank rolled his eyes and bit into the pastry.

"I was a little more interested in the mining," Joanna told Hank. "Did they ever pan for gold around here, in the Animas River, or someplace?"

"Animas," Hank mumbled, spewing a few crumbs as he spoke. "Yeah, there was gold in almost all of them rivers. Better color up north a little. Ouray River and such. I've heard tell of 'em panning the Animas, though."

"Where would they take the nuggets, though?" Joanna prompted. "Denver and Leadville didn't exist yet back then, right?"

Hank snorted, causing another shower of crumbs. "Nah, Cherry Creek, Leadville, none of 'em existed. There was a few little mining settlements not too far from Fort Ouray. Long way from Animas River, though. Long ways."

Joanna made her escape after a few minutes with a little help from Emma. She'd mostly found out what she wanted to know. The Animas River wasn't too far away. Maybe it was worth visiting. Maybe Latigo would be interested in that, she thought.

There was a tinkling sound from the bell as Hank left with his daughter. Emma mouthed the word *sorry* to Joanna on the way out. Joanna shook her head and waved. A man came in immediately after them, staring at Joanna as he took a seat. He had cruelty in his eyes and the lines around his mouth, Joanna thought. She took an instant dislike to him.

Miller pushed his way past crazy old Hank Brown and into the bakery. It was his first time in here, and the smell of fresh-baked bread and sweet rolls made him think he needed to come again.

He saw the server girl right away. Wallace hadn't done her justice, Miller decided. She was closer to beautiful than pretty, and Miller considered himself an expert. He had hired and fired dozens of girls at The

Rusty Bucket. This one was a blond with blue eyes. He had a weakness for blonds with blue eyes.

Miller passed a hand over his hair and sat down at a table. He turned on his best smile when the girl walked up to take his order. She said nothing, just stood with a pen and notebook, waiting.

"Hello, darlin'," Miller crooned, keeping the smile plastered on his face. "I'm Miller. You might have heard of The Rusty Bucket Saloon, down the street a little way? That's my place. Maybe you've been there?"

Joanna shook her head. "No, Mr. Miller, I've heard of your saloon, but I haven't been there. Not my kind of place, from what I've heard. Can I take your order?"

Miller's smile faded by a few notches. "Uh, bring me some coffee and two of your best sweet rolls. I think you'd like The Rusty Bucket if you came down there with me. It's lively. You could make the best tips in town if you worked down there with me."

Joanna shook her head again, this time with a little more emphasis. "I don't have any interest in leaving the bakery. I'll get your coffee and sweet rolls, Mr. Miller."

"Just Miller," he called after her. He felt the anger rising and forced himself to calm down. This wasn't the way he'd seen this going. She disappeared into the back and came out a few minutes later, placing the coffee cup and a plate of pastry on the table.

Miller reached out to take her hand, but she was too fast, retreating two steps and pulling her arm away. "Anything else, Mr. Miller?" she asked from a safe distance.

Miller shook his head impatiently and tried one more time. "I think you've got it all wrong, darlin'. You'd love it down at the saloon." He placed an extra dollar on the table, along with the money for his order.

Joanna turned toward the kitchen. "I'm not your darlin'. I thank you for the tip."

Miller noticed she hadn't reached for the tip. She was waiting for him to leave before she came to get it. He choked down the pastries and swilled the coffee, then left. He didn't want her to see how angry he was.

Miller reached the street and moved out of earshot before he turned loose a torrent of cursing. The little snip! He couldn't remember being treated like that. There wouldn't be a second time to let her make a fool of him. Again. This was about more than going through the girl to get to Latigo Smith now. This was personal.

TEN

RAIL YARD SHOOTOUT

Deacon strolled into his office/shack and took his usual seat. Matthew barely glanced up, then went back to work. Sometimes Deacon wondered if Matthew suspected the setup Deacon had going with Miller and Wallace. This kid, Matthew, didn't really seem curious about much of anything, though. That suited Deacon perfectly. He had enough trouble with his boss, Ward, looking over his shoulder all the time.

Glancing back to make sure he wasn't being watched, Deacon pulled the message from Matthew about the new shipment out of his pocket. The tools and supplies were coming in tonight on track number 8, in railcars 50 and 51. Estimated cost was $2,200. Deacon suppressed the low whistle he would have let loose if he were alone.

He shoved the note back into his pocket and thought about the arrangement and how it would play out tonight after his crew came in from the camp.

Deacon's opposite number at the Denver and Rio Grande Western was a guy he knew only as Cal. Miller had set things up directly with Cal. Deacon and had never laid eyes on Cal. He preferred it that way. Just take the money and spend it any way he wanted. Keep it simple.

The notes from Matthew, coming through Cal, always told him the track, cars, and value of the shipment. Deacon and his boys would take about half for his crew to use, building the rail line to Silverton. Stealing all of it would bring down the big boys. The money they kept for themselves, they would transfer to the track and cars given to him by Cal to be returned to Denver. There was always a note on the tools and supplies telling him where to transfer it.

Once Deacon and his boys had moved about half the shipment to the cars Cal specified, they would take the money for what they'd stolen from where Cal left it. The money was always on top of crates of tools, there in the railcar. The stolen tools would then go back to Denver, where Deacon figured Cal would use it for building one of their lines. Only after Cal's company had paid to buy a new shipment, of course. Deacon would split the stolen money three ways between himself, Miller, and Wallace. He was careful to split all of it. Miller scared him.

Deacon kept thinking about this latest message. He grabbed a pencil and some paper and did a little ciphering. The way he had it figured, tonight's job would be worth about twelve hundred dollars. He would pass out one hundred among his boys. Then he would have over three hundred and fifty for one night's work.

This was too much to think about without a little celebration. He would go to the café and treat himself to breakfast, then over to The Rusty Bucket when it opened. Not too much whiskey, he cautioned himself. He had to be sober tonight.

━━━

Holt and I got ready to go just as soon as we'd grabbed some dinner. Holt picked up his Winchester and shotgun and looked at me. "Winchester or Ole Betsy?" he asked. "Or both?"

"Both," I told him.

Holt chuckled. "Only thing you know how to do better than start a fight is how to end a fight. I love it."

I walked over and found Buck sitting on a log, finishing up his dinner. I motioned for him to come with me.

Buck followed, keeping a safe distance and watching me. He didn't look mad. He just looked curious. That was good. Sometimes, two guys could have been in a knockdown, drag-out fight with no hard feelings afterward. I was hoping this was one of those times.

"I need to go into town tonight, me and Holt," I told him. "I need you to be in charge here. Don't let 'em fight with each other. Get 'em ready for work tomorrow if I ain't back by breakfast. Will you do that?"

Buck stared at me like it was just a big trick. He

waited for me to say something else. Finally, he blinked a couple times, shifted his feet, and said, "Yeah, I'll do it."

"Good," I said. "I'll go tell the boys they'll answer to you for the next day."

"Wait!" Buck's voice stopped me before I'd taken two steps.

"Why are you doin' this? I was ready to take yore head off yesterday."

"Yeah, we had us a donnybrook," I agreed. I touched my sore ribs. "I got kicked in the ribs by a mule one time and it didn't hurt much more than that punch you landed yesterday." I stared at the ground for a minute and got serious.

"A very smart man, good friend of mine, once taught me that sometimes you gotta trust your gut and give a man a chance. Put your trust in 'em, and maybe they'll live up to it. Both of you come out better off. I'm trusting you. Maybe you just got some bad advice the other day. Maybe today you've got a better idea of who to trust."

Buck shifted his feet and slowly nodded his head. "Yeah," he said, "mebbe I do."

I walked over and rang the dinner triangle next to Cookie's fire. "Listen up," I hollered. The boys quieted down. "I'm gonna be gone tonight, maybe till sometime tomorrow morning. Buck is in charge. You don't answer to him, you'll have to answer to me."

There was a little buzz while they talked that one over. I nodded at Buck, then walked over and mounted up. Holt and I were hoping to reach Durango before sundown. We needed to rustle up a little firepower.

Holt and I pulled up in front of the jailhouse with just a little daylight left in the western skies. We walked inside and found Marshal Anderson there, along with Cleo Ward. I looked at Ward in surprise. "What are you doing here?" I blurted.

Ward grinned. "I knew there was gonna be some hot times tonight, Smith. You can't leave me out of this." He turned and lifted a rifle, leaning against the desk behind him. "I've got this Spencer, and I know how to use it. During the war and after. I'm in."

I nodded. "Glad to have you." I turned to Anderson. "Wallace ain't here—that's good," I said. "Where is he?"

Anderson shrugged. "Sometimes he's just gone for a day or two. I don't always know where. Anyhow, you told Ward not to fill him in on this, right?" He looked troubled. I would have to tell him about my suspicions later.

"Right." I looked around. "Okay, we've got surprise and four guns against maybe five. We need to get set up over at the rail yard." I led the way out.

We hitched our horses a few blocks away from the train yard and came the rest of the way on foot. I wanted the horses available in case we had to chase anybody down, but I didn't want the thieves to see the horses and get scared off.

There was nobody watching the yard. I was a little surprised at that, but Ward just shrugged. "Didn't think we needed anybody watching this place up until now," he told me.

I found track number eight, then railcars 50 and 51. "These are the ones," I murmured.

The marshal stared at me. "How would you know that?" he asked.

"There's nothing in these cars," I said. "I set this thing up with a message to Deacon."

Anderson sighed. "So, Deacon is in on this. I guess Deputy Wallace is too?"

"I think so." I looked at the setup we had here. There was another track, number nine, running alongside number eight, about twenty-five yards away. The doors to cars 50 and 51 faced this track. On the far side of track eight, there were stacks of crates and a couple of old train cars that didn't look like they'd been anywhere in a while. We needed to make everything happen on this side of track eight. I didn't want to be chasing anybody around in the dark among all those crates and old rail cars.

I looked at the cars over on track nine. They were boxcars with a roof running along the top. "High ground wins," I mumbled to myself. "Marshal Anderson," I said, "could you and Ward climb up on top of those cars over there? I'm hoping everybody surrenders all peaceful-like, but if they don't, Holt and me will need some backing fire from you."

I pulled the watch from my pocket. It was eleven

o'clock now. If I were them, I thought, I'd do this in the middle of the night. "Everybody get as comfortable as you can," I told them. "We might be waitin' for a while out here."

I took a closer look at the doors on cars fifty and fifty-one while Ward and Anderson climbed up over on track nine. They weren't locked. I had a feeling Deacon had himself a confederate with the rival train line, smoothing his way on this thing, so maybe this would look normal to him.

I went over with Holt and ducked down into the shadows of the cars on track nine, just waiting in the darkness. It was colder than I'd expected. I had to fight down the urge to stamp my feet to get the blood flowing.

If you stare into the shadows long enough, you start to see things. After maybe an hour, I thought I saw some of those shadows moving. When I heard the squeal of those doors opening, I knew I hadn't imagined. Next thing I knew, somebody had lit up a lantern over in front of car 50. They had to see well enough to move the stuff. I hadn't counted on that, but it helped us a considerable amount.

I moved up to a half-crouch, my Winchester out in front of me. "Hold on, boys," I barked. "Nobody move." My voice carried and bounced around in that train yard, and for just a second, I thought they were gonna do what I said. Then some fool pulled his hogleg out of his holster and threw the lantern toward the sound of my voice.

Gunfire erupted. I raised the Winchester and fired at the first man, who was climbing up into the railcar.

Shots sounded from above me, that would be Anderson and Ward opening fire. Bullets were pinging off the cars behind me, at least a couple of those boys got their pistols out and opened fire.

The smell of gunpowder hung heavy in the air. I cocked the Winchester and looked for another target, then Holt cut loose with both barrels of his shotgun. After the echoes died down, there was nothing.

I advanced across the way with Holt on my wing. I could hear Anderson and Ward scrambling down from the top of the railcar behind us. We reached car fifty and found three men down—dead or dying. Two had taken rifle shots through the chest. A shotgun blast had hit the third. He was a mess. I looked and saw a fourth man, down on his knees with his hands in the air. The shotgun blast had cut him up a little— had some pellets in his shoulder, it looked like, but he would make it. Anderson took him prisoner.

I looked around me. Four men accounted for, but I was pretty sure I'd seen five in the light of that lantern before we fired all the shots. Then I heard a sound that could only be boots running on wood. Somebody had gotten under the train and was running down the side of the track on the other side of track eight.

I crawled under number fifty and came out on the other side. I could hear those boots a lot more clearly now, pounding the wooden planks as somebody ran down the track. This was exactly what I hadn't wanted —a shootout in the dark.

There was just a bit of light from a quarter-moon overhead. I could see his outline, dashing straight down the tracks, half-hidden by the shadow of the train. I dropped to one knee and pulled my Colt, steadying down and locking in on that moving shadow. I squeezed the trigger. He staggered off the tracks, half crouched over, and moved behind a pile of crates.

"Lat?" That was Holt, still on the other side of the train. I didn't need somebody else over here in the dark—we might just shoot each other. "Stay on that side," I told him. "I've got this."

A shot whistled over my head and ricocheted off car number fifty. I didn't know if he could see my shadow or if he just fired toward the voice, but this place was too hot to stick around. I crouched over and sprinted to duck behind the shadow of an abandoned rail car.

I strained to pick up any sound in the darkness but heard nothing. Maybe he was moving like a cat out there, maybe I'd hurt him and he had to stay put, or maybe he was just waiting for me to come to him.

I stayed put for about a minute, listening and deciding what to do. Staying here went against my nature. I would take the fight to him. Moving along the train track seemed like a bad idea. That's where I'd be watching if I were him.

Decision made, I came out from behind the train car and moved to flank him on the far side. There were piles of crates and another old rail car or two to shield me. I moved about thirty yards to the far side of where I figured he was, then stopped to reload my pistol. I might need all those shots.

Now I turned to my right and worked my way closer to him. When I thought I was about even with his position, I dropped and crawled, using whatever junk was out there to shield me.

Coming even with a pile of crates, I held my breath and peeked around the corner. I could see him now, down on his knees with his back to a pile of crates, outlined by the moonlight. He was holding a shoulder with one hand, but his pistol was out. He was looking the other way, toward the train.

"Easy does it," I said, my voice carrying across the yard. "I've got you in my sights. It's over. No point in gettin' all shot up."

He turned his head slowly in my direction. It was Deacon. No surprise there.

"Latigo Smith," he growled. "I shoulda never hired you. You was much too curious and pushy. Ward made me hire somebody." He coughed and moaned. His hand dropped away from his shoulder.

For just a minute, I thought he was going to drop his gun. His gun hand moved toward the ground, but then he spun in my direction and jerked it up. That must have hurt, 'cause he howled.

I fired twice, one right after the other, holding steady on the middle of his chest. He spilled sideways and backward. The pile of crates came down on top of him. I could just see his feet now, sticking out from under them. As I advanced on the crates, I could see his pistol lying to the side.

I pulled the crates aside. Deacon was on his back, just staring up. I closed his eyes and stood. "I got him, boys," I called. "This is over."

They came around the end of the train and walked back to join me. Marshal Anderson had the prisoner's hands tied up. He and Ward took a look at the body on the ground.

"You were right," Anderson nodded. "Deacon." He told us he would arrange for some folks to bury the bodies the next day and walked his prisoner back toward the jail.

Ward fell in beside me as we left the train yard. "I knew you must be right about Deacon, just didn't want to believe it..." his voice trailed off. "Well, I guess it's over, Smith, as far as the robberies, I mean. Maybe tomorrow I can talk to you about finishing this railroad to Silverton."

"There's one more thing you'll probably want to look into," I said. "Deacon must have had him a partner over there with the Denver & Rio Grande Western. This stealing was just way too easy."

Ward thought it over and nodded. "I'll look into it," he agreed. "What about this Deputy Marshal Wallace?"

"Yeah," I said. "I've still got to talk to Anderson about that." We reached the horses and decided we'd all done enough for one day. Holt and I went to find a room in town. I had a couple things to square up before we went back to the railroad camp tomorrow sometime.

Holt and I mounted up, and I led the way to the boarding house I knew Joanna was using.

━━━

"What's gonna happen out at the railroad camp?" Holt asked me as we stepped up on the porch.

I shook my head. "Don't know. Ward wants to talk to me about it tomorrow. I'm sure they'll still need somebody to bring in meat for the crew. Not sure if they need me anymore, though. Deacon and those four guys were behind it. That's all wrapped up."

Holt stopped on the porch and looked up at the boarding house sign. His eyes turned suspicious. "Is this where that purty girl Joanna is stayin'?"

I shrugged and lied through my teeth. "I dunno." I pushed on into the lobby.

Holt snorted and followed me in.

We pushed on into the lobby of the place. There was a lantern burning on a desk and a note:

> *If you cum in late and need a room,*
> *this here is the key to number eight.*
> *Make sure you ain't to drunk to find*
> *number eight. Thats gonna be two*
> *bits in the mawnin.*
> *Zeke.*

I took the key and looked at Holt. "There's just gonna be one bed, you know," I told him. Holt snorted and went looking for number eight. "I'll sleep on the floor, pard. You gotta pay him the two bits."

ELEVEN
NEW BOSS

Miller stood outside the clapboard house he'd bought when he first opened The Rusty Bucket in Durango. He was just a couple blocks off Main Street, close enough to walk the few blocks to his saloon, far enough away that the drunk miners didn't keep him awake at night.

Miller wandered down to Main Street, drinking his first coffee of the morning and scratching himself irritably. Normally, he didn't hear any guns going off in town. His snoring probably drowned out the sound. Last night, though, was different. Somebody, or several somebodies, had cut loose with gunfire in the middle of the night. He hadn't gone out to look. That was a good way to catch a stray bullet.

Now he could see an old fleabag of a horse pulling a cart down the street. He knew that horse. It belonged to Tyson, the old barber who also served as the undertaker. That cart was likely headed for boot hill. Instantly, Miller was interested. This meant those shots last night weren't just some drunk miners letting off some steam. Somebody had hit what they shot at.

Miller moved closer to Main Street, trying not to look too interested. He had a reputation around town as a saloon owner who served up the whiskey and minded his own business, and that's the way he wanted to keep it. At least with most people, he had that reputation. He discouraged the folks who wanted to say anything else about him.

When he reached Main Street, he turned his head to look at the cart. They were carrying coffins, all right, four of them. They looked like Tyson's cheapest pine board coffins, barely holding the corpses inside, probably. That meant these dead guys weren't special to anybody. Or at least nobody wanted the town to know about it if they were.

Seeing Marshal Anderson following the cart on foot, Miller gave him a halfhearted wave and went back to his house. Wallace had been out there with Anderson at the sheriff's office, most likely, so Miller would get any news he needed in about an hour when he met with Wallace in the room at the back of The Rusty Bucket. Deacon, too, if he hadn't gone back to the railroad camp already.

An hour and a half and two coffees later, Miller's hands were drumming a steady tattoo on the top of the table in his office. What was the holdup? Deacon might have gone back to the camp, but Wallace should have been here a half hour ago.

Another fifteen minutes and Miller was thinking about switching to whiskey when the door opened and Wallace came in. He took a seat without making eye contact. That was a bad sign.

"Where's Deacon?" Miller demanded. "Back at the camp? Who were those dead guys in the coffins out there? Somebody was shootin' up the town last night, down at the other end of Main Street, it sounded like."

Wallace leaned forward in his chair, waving away coffee when a server came into the room.

"Git," Miller growled at her. She fled.

"Deacon ain't gonna make it," Wallace announced. Miller bored in with his stare. Wallace looked sideways. "Deacon was one of the dead guys in the coffins," he murmured in a low tone. "Two others were from the rail crew that helped Deacon move the stuff. They taken one prisoner. There's another one. Tyson ain't done with him yet, on account he needs more time to patch him up enough to plant him. He was torn up."

Miller shoved his chair and began to pace back and forth in the tiny backroom. Wallace hadn't seen him pacing before. He wasn't sure if it was good or bad, but he was pretty sure it was bad. He decided to shut his mouth and wait it out.

When Miller came back to the table, his face was flushed, but he was quiet and under control. Wallace thought back to a mule he'd owned a long time ago. If the mule got quiet and laid his ears back, you didn't want to mess with it. This might be like that mule. Wallace held his tongue and waited.

Miller was staring at the back wall, but there was

nobody there. Wallace checked to make sure, then turned around to listen. "Get out to the rail camp," Miller said. "I need to know what happened out there. Is this Buck guy in charge now? Where is Latigo Smith? What's he doing? I need him cleared out of the picture. Find out what's going on at the camp, then come right back. I'm gonna have a plan by then."

Wallace nodded, shoved his chair back, and started for the door. A thought struck him and he turned back. "What about the bakery girl? Do you still want me to find out more about her?"

Miller shook his head and waved a hand in the air. His mouth closed down into a thin line. "Let me worry about that bakery girl," he snarled.

Wallace jammed his hat on his head and made his escape. He'd never seen Miller keeping himself under tight control like this. He had a feeling this was Miller's most dangerous mood.

━━━

We cantered out of town after a fast stop at Ma's Bakery. Ma had shoved a huge plate of food under Holt's nose, then gave him a bag of more food when we left. I talked to Joanna for a while, then shook my head when Ma gave the bag of food to Holt.

"You know what happens when you feed a stray, don't you, Ma?" I asked.

Ma just chuckled. "That boy needs to keep his strength up. Besides, he's gonna bring me some elk backstrap. Maybe some more meat I could use to make breakfast sausage. It's a good trade."

We said our goodbyes, and now Holt was giving me the business about Joanna. I just ignored him as best I could. It was like a skeeter buzzin' around your ear, though. Hard to forget about it.

Joanna had been telling me about an old codger named Hank Brown who'd been a trapper back in the 1830s, back when her grandfather and my uncle were runnin' pelts to Los Angeles. Hank Brown had talked about some panning done in the Animas River, and did I think maybe that's where somebody could have found the black pellets? Maybe that's where Ezekiel had seen some before?

It sounded a lot closer to Durango than I'd have thought, but I promised to think about it some more and see if I could take a ride up there. I'd not been to the Animas River.

Then there was the quick meeting with Cleo Ward, who had come by just as we were leaving the boarding house. He said he didn't have time to talk right now but wanted to come out to the rail camp in a couple hours to talk to me.

Holt burst in on my line of thought. "Whaddya think Mr. Ward wants to talk about?"

I shrugged and pulled my hat down a little lower. "Don't know," I admitted. "He's gotta be wondering how he's gonna get this track on through to Silverton without Deacon. Deacon was runnin' both ends, out at the camp and back in Durango."

"Yeah, plus runnin' all the stealing back at the train tracks," Holt added.

I couldn't help but laugh. "Yeah, that too. At least Ward won't have to worry about that anymore.

Maybe Matthew can help out a little more back at that office."

"Ward wants you to run things at the camp. He's gonna ask you to be the foreman out here."

I turned in my saddle to stare at him. "I don't know how to be a foreman on a rail line," I burst out, louder than I'd planned. "Don't know nuthin' about it. He'd be crazy."

"Buck knows that stuff. He can tell 'em. You just got to work with the engineers or whoever they've got to tell you where the tracks go. I'll bet ole Buck would like workin' for you more than workin' for Deacon. You tell Buck and he tells them. You can jest put yer feet up on the saddle and think about that purty girl back at the bakery."

We were back to that. I just shut up, and we were done talking till we got back to the camp.

When we got there, it looked like Holt had it right, at least the part about Buck taking care of things. He had split them up in their teams, measuring and marking the ties, with the other group laying 'em down. They were hard at it, with Buck in the middle of it. He stopped and lifted a hand at me. I waved back and rode over to rejoin Holt. Might as well let the boys keep working.

Holt was checking his Winchester and stuffing a box of ammo in his saddlebags. He glanced overhead at the sun. "Too late to catch any deer feeding," he muttered. "Might catch one or two coming for water. If not, I'll get something at sundown and Cookie will have to work out supper with these boys with whatever he's got." He grinned at me. "You can tell Cookie that part. Don't tell him if he's got him a frying pan in his hands," he advised.

I decided to leave off telling Cookie anything until later on. I stowed my Winchester at my campsite and started to wonder what to do with myself. I didn't have to worry about catching people robbing the supplies out here anymore. I found myself staring at a couple of mesas I could see off in the distance. I wondered if one of those was where old Barnabus Smith had found the black pebbles.

"You don't have to worry about folks stealing the supplies anymore." Ward's voice startled me. I had to remember he'd been in the army and could sneak up on me if he wanted to, when I wasn't paying attention.

I grinned. "Yeah, I kinda did what you hired me for."

Ward dismounted and led his horse over, then tethered him to a log. He pointed at another log and took a seat. "Let's talk," he said.

I took a seat, and Ward got right down to it. "I want you to run this crew, just like Deacon used to do," he blurted.

That one put me back on my haunches, even though Holt had just got done tellin' me this was gonna happen. "I don't know how to run the railroad crew," I objected. "Ain't never done this kind of thing before."

Ward just swatted that one away as soon as I said it. "Two things you gotta do. Just talk with the engineers from time to time and take their advice on where to lay the tracks. They'll have it planned out. Second thing is to keep the men told off on what they need to do and make sure they do it. Buck can help you with that."

I hemmed and hawed and stalled for a while. Fact is, I was worried I couldn't do a good job. Ward jumped in and closed the deal.

"What was I paying you before? What you and Deacon agreed on, I mean."

"Two dollars an' twenty-five cents a day," I told him. "Because I was doin' special work for him."

"I'll pay three for you to be the foreman."

Well now, that sounded right nice, but I kept my poker face on. It felt like this whole thing was getting away from me. "I gotta talk to Buck first," I said.

Ward stood up, walked a few steps, stuck his fingers in his mouth, and cut loose the loudest whistle I'd ever heard. He waved his arms in the air. "Buck!" he shouted.

Buck dropped what he was doing and trotted right over.

"Buck," Ward said, putting an arm around his shoulders. "I just told Lat Smith, here, that I want him to be the foreman around this place, but I want you to help him out, just like you did with Deacon. That okay, with you?"

Buck looked over at me, and his face was pretty messed up. One eye was still swole about halfway shut, and his mouth was pretty puffed up, too. His face had purple bruises all over it. "I'd like it just fine, probly better than workin' for Deacon," he nodded.

"Done," Ward said. "I'm raising your pay to two dollars a day for this."

Buck grinned and trotted back to the crew. Ward

watched him leave, then shook his head and chuckled. "I'm bettin' you put those bruises on his face," he said, "but you boys seem to have it worked out. We're good here?"

I nodded and said nothing about Buck's face. Ward walked over and mounted up. "I'll have Matthew do a little more at the office, and I'll help him out a little more. You just need to keep it moving here. I'll be back and introduce you to the engineers in a couple of days." He touched his heels to the horse and trotted away.

I stood and watched him disappear down the tracks, looked around, and shook my head. Just like Holt had called it. Railroad foreman. Who'd have thought it?

———

Wallace sat his horse for a while longer, hidden within a stand of pine trees. He put his field glasses away and stroked his beard while he thought. Lat Smith and Ward had been shootin' the breeze for a long time down there, and it looked to him like Ward had talked Smith into something. Deacon's job would be his guess.

Wallace heaved a deep sigh. Deacon in a pine box meant their sweet deal stealing from the railroad was over. Buck had been over there talking, too. What did that mean? Wallace was shocked at what Buck's face had looked like. Just about like a side of beef. Looked like Smith was good with his fists.

Wallace reined his horse around and retraced his

trail to Durango. Time to report to Miller. He wasn't looking forward to it.

━━━

Joanna paused on the steps of a small house. Weather-beaten, unpainted boards surrounded an uneven roof with a chimney and stovepipe sticking out the top. There was a wide porch running the length of the front of the house, with a well-used swing hanging from the rafters. Several flower boxes were in the two front windows, boasting a colorful array of flowers.

Joanna shifted her picnic basket, full of the muffins old Hank Brown liked the best, along with some of Ma Barker's best coffee. She climbed the creaky front steps, knocked on the door, and waited. She was a little nervous. Emma had made a passing comment about coming to see them, but Joanna had to go to Ma to get their address.

She could hear steps coming to the door now, then Emma was framed in the doorway. Hank's head poked out from behind his daughter. His eyes were glued to the picnic basket. "Is that some of them muffins I'm partial to?" he bellowed. Emma winced at the booming voice in her ear, then pulled the door open and waved Joanna inside.

Emma led the way to a table in the small kitchen. Hank trailed along behind, careful not to get too far away from the muffins. They took a seat while Emma got out cups and poured coffee for everybody while Hank attacked the muffins.

After Emma cleared the plates away, Hank shot a

knowing glance at Joanna. "I expect you've come to find out what else you can about yer grandpappy, haven't you, young lady? Glad you came here—I didn't wanna talk anymore at the bakery."

Joanna nodded.

Hank chuckled. "Yeah, they was plannin' to pan for gold at the Animas. They done some panning there a few times. Mostly they panned in the Ouray River, though. They was goin' on to Los Angeles with some pelts this time, they was. Never saw 'em again after that trip."

Hank smacked his lips a couple times and stared at the muffins on the kitchen counter. Emma had laid the three remaining muffins on a plate and brought the picnic basket back to Joanna. Emma shook her finger at her dad and Hank heaved a deep sigh.

Now he shifted his glance to Joanna. "There was a story, kinda made the rounds, about old Barnabus Smith and Zeke Dunne, maybe finding some gold. They talked about Barnabus Smith and the gold nuggets up on a mesa top. Never set much store by it, myself. Word is that old Barnabus went lookin' for that mesa, years after, and never found it. That's all I ever heard."

Joanna reached out to place a hand on Hank's wrist. "Thank you, Hank. You knew what I wanted to ask about before I ever got the question out." She hesitated and looked over at Emma. "There's just one other thing I wondered about. Somebody was in the bakery that morning, and he, well...he scares me."

"Clem Miller." The words burst out of Hank's mouth and his face clouded over. "Don't know much about him, but his daddy was with us, back in them days. Leroy Miller. Panned the Ouray River and trapped beaver with us. Liar and a cheat, he was. Probly a killer, too."

Hank's face went red, and he mumbled to himself, shifting in the rickety old kitchen chair. Emma stood and hovered over him anxiously.

Joanna was sorry she'd asked. She got to her feet and looked at the two of them. "I'm sorry, I shouldn't have asked about that." She gathered the picnic basket to leave. Hank reached out to grab her arm.

"Don't you worry yore head about it, young lady. Only right to know who you trust an' who you don't. I'll tell you this much. Leroy Miller used to take the pelts to a tradin' post out east of us. Taken a few gold nuggets, too. Lied about how much we got every time, that's what I'm thinkin'. Only didn't nobody want to complain too much. Word is that were a good way to get a knife in yore ribs while yore sleeping."

Feeling bad at how much she'd upset old Hank, Joanna took her basket and moved toward the door after a few more minutes. Emma saw her out.

"Don't worry about Dad," she said. "He'll calm down and be himself in a few more minutes." She looked over her shoulder. "We don't know a lot about Clem Miller from dealing with him ourselves," she said in a low murmur. "But the word is, he's a lot worse than his daddy ever was."

TWELVE
PLANS MADE

Joanna felt rooted to the porch as Emma's words struck home. It's what she had feared, but now she knew she wasn't entirely prepared to hear it. Her instincts were right—Miller was a dangerous man, and, for some reason, he had zeroed in on her.

She shot a glance sideways at Emma, who was looking up and down the street to see if they were being watched. Joanna moved down the steps of the porch.

Emma reached out to grab her arm. "No," she said, "you don't have to run off. There's nobody watching us."

Joanna moved back up to the porch. She wanted to look up and down the street too, but she forced herself not to do it. "Can you tell me anything else? It seems like Miller wants to single me out for his attention." She crossed her arms. "Why would he do that? And what makes him so dangerous?"

Emma shook her head. "I don't know why he

would pay so much attention to you, unless it has to do with Miller's father and your grandfather and the trapping and panning they did back then. You would know as much about that as me. As to why he's dangerous..."

Emma stopped, bit her lip, and looked around one more time. "You can't talk about this with anybody else unless it's for your own protection. It's pretty common knowledge that Miller runs a gang of high-waymen all over western Colorado. Most of the gold fever and mining has died down, but it hasn't been safe to carry nuggets or gold dust for a long time. Nobody in town will talk about it because it isn't safe, and nobody is ready to stand up to Miller."

Emma stopped and gathered her breath, clearly deciding whether she wanted to go on. Joanna just waited. She was prepared to leave if Emma didn't feel safe telling her the rest.

The door opened, and Hank stuck his head out. He looked back and forth at the two women. "Everything okay?" he asked.

Emma nodded, and Hank went back inside. "There's something else," Emma went on. "Word has it that Miller has ties to a renegade Ute warrior who has himself a war party out there somewhere. The Ute chief is Chief Ouray, and he's peaceable. The renegade is Severo, and he's been on the warpath from time to time. Dad thinks there's a tie going back to childhood between Severo and Miller. And he thinks maybe Miller is behind some of Severo's raids...that's just Dad's opinion, but he was around back then."

Joanna could sense Emma's growing discomfort.

She moved back down the steps and turned. "Thank you for telling me. I can keep a secret." She paused. "I have a friend. He's running railroad security for the line from Durango to Silverton, and I trust him."

"You can tell him. Just him. What's his name? Durango could use a man strong enough to stand up to Miller."

"His name is Latigo Smith. I'll introduce you sometime when you're both down at the bakery." She moved away.

"Both of you, be careful," Emma murmured.

Joana moved down to the street and made a sudden decision not to take a straight path back to the bakery. It was just a hunch, but she walked away from Main Street for two blocks, then turned left for several blocks before turning left again to return to Main Street. She came in from the other side of the bakery and went back in to resume her day. She didn't see Miller lurking at a corner three blocks down the street.

———

Ward came out with the engineers just a couple days later. He introduced them, but I forgot their names right away, of course. I was too busy staring at the maps they laid out on a table in a tent we set up. Those maps were scary.

One guy stayed with us to help. His name was Jones. I called him Jonesy. Jones knew where we were goin' and he seemed to know how to get there. Those maps and the engineers told me we had to go over two or three peaks, mebbe nine thousand feet high, and blast our way through a couple more. We had to cross the Animas River three times.

They showed me all that stuff on the map, then sat back and looked at me. Ward asked me if I had any questions. I looked over at Jones. "You're sticking around to help, right, Jonesy?"

He grinned and nodded. Ward guffawed and fired up a big cigar. "Jonesy, I like that. You boys are gonna get along. What else, Lat?"

I had to get my bearings. "How long is this track gonna be, Durango to Silverton?"

Ward leaned back and blew a gigantic cloud of smoke at the top of the tent. "Forty-eight miles altogether. We've built nigh onto eleven miles so far. It's gonna go a lot faster now that we don't have Deacon and his boys stealing all our stuff. Lat took care of that," he said to the engineers.

"How long do you figger this is gonna take to finish?" I asked.

Ward looked at Jonesy. Jonesy locked his hands behind his head and stared at the map. "Let's see," he mumbled. "We've been at it almost three months, but we're almost over Red Mountain Pass. I'd say, six more months," he said.

I stood up to walk around. Sometimes I have to walk when my head is doing some ciphering. "It's May," I said. "Six months put us into...uh, November." I looked around at Jonesy. "Snow's gonna be flying by the time we get to Silverton," I pointed out.

Jonesy grinned. "It's gonna be cold. We can do it."

Everybody else decided the meeting was over, I

guess. Ward walked over and clapped me on the shoulder. "I'll be out ever' few days," he said. "I'm gonna headquarter right here in Durango for a while." He turned serious. "This is important, Lat. There's a lot of gold and silver comin' out of those hills up in Silverton. The railroad is how it gets to market. No highwaymen, no holdups. Just nice and safe, down the railroad."

They all mounted up and rode back to town. Except for Jonesy. I turned around to look at him. "I hope you know what you're doin', Jonesy."

He grinned and nodded. "I know. We just got to keep the supplies flowing now, and you've gotta keep 'em working. We'll get there."

━━━

Miller had been waiting in the back room for a while. Wallace could tell by the amount of cigar smoke hanging in the air. That and the number of empty whiskey glasses. He took a seat without saying anything. Miller was staring at the back wall again.

"Tell me about this guy, Buck, at the camp." Miller was still staring off into the distance, but Wallace knew he was the only one in the room. He glanced at the whiskey glasses on the table, they were all empty. He hoped that meant Miller had quit drinking for a while. One of these days, they were probably going to face off. He hoped it wasn't today.

"Buck's been beat to a pulp. Face is just one big purple bruise. Got one eye all swole up. Probly can't see out of it. Looks pretty clear this Latigo Smith guy is running the railroad out there now. He must be the one that left Buck all stove up."

"Hmmph. Latigo Smith again." It came out as a growl, but Miller wasn't drunk. "I paid one of them waitresses at the café, one of 'em that takes food to the guys in jail…" Miller trailed off and stared at the wall some more. "Anyhow, I paid her to pretend she was that guy's girl, the one they taken prisoner at the rail yard. She taken the food back to his cell. That marshal, Anderson, he let her talk to him at the cell."

Miller stopped and snorted. "What a fool. Anyhow, she tole him I'll give him some money when he gits out, and to tell her who done all the shootin' at the rail yard." Miller shook his head. "He's a fool, too. They'll probly hang him."

Miller got up and started pacing. "He says this Latigo Smith guy kilt Deacon. Shot him to doll rags." He stopped pacing and dropped back into his chair. "That means I've got me a score to settle with this here Latigo Smith."

Miller shifted and fixed a stare on Wallace. "You said Latigo Smith is runnin' the railroad operation now."

Wallace nodded. "Looks like it, yeah."

Miller grunted. "Ain't gonna do no good to offer him a deal like Deacon. Gonna have to take him outta the way first, afore we kin do anything else. Maybe git the railroad scairt enough to pay us for some protection."

Wallace had a feeling Miller had already thought this one out. His stomach turned over. He had a feeling he was about to have to tell Miller no.

"You heard of Severo, right?" The question startled Wallace. "Renegade Ute warrior, made some raids on White folk here and there." Wallace nodded.

"I know Severo," Miller blurted. "Done business with him a time or two. Injuns always need rifles, ammo, mebbe a little firewater. You're gonna work with him, guide him to where they're workin' on the railroad and such."

"Nope." Wallace was startled at how steady his voice was. "My deal is I'm the deppity marshal, lettin' you know what's happenin', keepin' the law off your back. If I'm caught workin' with Severo, that's all gonna be over."

Miller was stunned. Wallace could see it in his eyes. Wallace was watching those eyes. Miller must just draw and fire under the table. His right hand inched closer to his Colt. They stared each other down for several seconds.

Miller leaned back and smiled a thin, cruel smile. He leaned his head back and roared. "Mouse!"

A kid stuck his head through the door and came in carrying another shot of whiskey. He set it on the table and turned to leave. Wallace had seen this kid around The Rusty Bucket. Bruised up just like Buck, the first time he'd seen this kid.

Miller spoke to Mouse, but his eyes never left Wallace. "We're ridin' out to see a warrior named Severo, Mouse. You're gonna learn where to meet up with him, take him some guns and ammo and fire-water time to time. Leavin' now. All of us."

Miller's eyes challenged Wallace as he rose slowly. Wallace glanced at the kid, Mouse, his mouth was hanging open in surprise. Wallace nodded and stood. He'd go along with this much. He would ride out to meet this Severo.

Miller left off staring at Wallace and led the way out of the back room, followed by Mouse, who was still stunned. Wallace trailed behind them. He was pretty sure now he would wind up shooting it out with Miller one of these days. He wasn't sure who would win. At least, he thought, it didn't look like it would be today.

One good thing about the miles of track already laid— Ward could send supplies and bags of beans and such out on handcarts. It took two boys pumping pretty hard, but they were used to it. I found out I could leave Buck in charge and get a free ride back to town once in a while. I would generally stop in to talk to Ward a bit, but then I always wound up at Ma's Bakery.

Joanna was surprised, but I figured it was a good sign she hugged me when I walked in and brought me a free muffin and coffee. "The coffee is on Ma," she said, "the muffin is on me." She pulled out a chair and sat down.

I had a lot to tell her about the shootout at the rail yard and how I was in charge at the camp now. I told her about the route we would take to Silverton. I saw how her eyes lit up when I said we would cross the Animas River three times.

She leaned in and lowered her voice. "I went to see

an old trapper and miner named Hank Brown," she said. "He knew your uncle and my grandfather. I think maybe people did some panning in the Animas River back then. Maybe that's where somebody originally found those black pebbles. Maybe my uncles saw some there, too." She looked around and started to say more, but then Cleo Ward walked in.

"The handcart came back this mornin' and they said you were on it," he boomed. "Knew I'd find you down here."

I pushed out a chair for him, and he took a seat. He took off his hat and grinned at Joanna. "Knew I'd find you here," he repeated. "I'm surprised I haven't seen Joanna out at the camp," he joked.

She looked at me. "Maybe I could come out sometime," she said.

I started to shake my head no, but Ma showed up with some coffee for Ward. "I'll bet those boys might like to buy some fresh-baked bread and pies out there," she said.

Ward's head came up. "They'd buy everything you've got in five minutes," he promised. "Even if you doubled your price."

Ma looked back and forth at Joanna and me. "It seems to me maybe she could go out with you on the handcart and sell a lot of bread and pies for me." She grinned.

I didn't seem to have anything to say. I looked over at Ward. He grinned again. "Just make sure you have a loaf of bread and a pie for everybody there." He chuckled. "Otherwise, you and Buck and Holt all put together will never get those boys calmed down."

Ward stayed a while longer and I said I would meet him back at the office. Joanna leaned back in and told me what she'd learned about a guy named Miller who owned The Rusty Bucket Saloon and how he was paying way too much attention to her.

I sat back and listened until she finished. Ma came by and told Joanna she needed her in the back.

Joanna nodded and stood to follow Ma to the kitchen. She leaned in and squeezed my shoulder. "I'll be careful," she said, "but come back and see me as soon as you can."

She disappeared into the back. I watched her go. Sometimes, I get a bad feeling way down in my gut, and this was one of those times. Ma's terrific breakfast didn't seem so good all of a sudden.

They rode out just a few hours before dusk, leaving one at a time. Miller went first. He had a Winchester 73 and a bottle of whiskey strapped on his saddle and covered over with a blanket. He intended those to be gifts to Severo, with a promise of more for his warriors. First, Miller wanted to see some raids on the railroad from Severo's band.

Mouse rode out about a half hour later, followed by Wallace, bringing up the rear. Wallace had told his boss, Marshal Anderson, that he was going to scout the railroad progress. That was kinda true, he told himself, but Anderson didn't look like he was buying what Wallace was selling. That could be a problem.

Wallace had some doubts about all of this. It had

gone from a sweet business deal to raids on the rail-road. Railroads had a funny way of fighting back. They didn't like having their lines attacked, and those railroads had some experience with this.

Miller said they were staying overnight in Severo's camp as a show they meant business and weren't scared of Severo. That sounded like another bad idea. Wallace had to admit he was nervous about it. Mouse was terrified. Wallace could see it on his face before they left.

They met up about an hour north of Durango. The high, flat plains of Durango were lifting toward some mountain peaks up ahead of them. Miller claimed to know where Severo's camp was and said they only had another hour to go. If that wasn't true, it would be dark, and they would have to make camp. That was something else Wallace didn't like.

The trail widened before the sharp climb began. Wallace spurred his horse even with Miller and lifted the blanket to look at the Winchester 73. He dropped the blanket. "You sure that Winchester's a good idea? You could just give 'em a few more old Henrys and Spencers like they've got now."

Miller grunted. "Severo might know the difference. Anyway, I ain't gonna give 'em all Winchesters. Just Severo and mebbe a couple others. The ones that ain't got rifles right now will be plenty happy with an old Spencer or something. I'm gonna go easy on the fire-water, too. Don't want those boys too drunk to attack."

Wallace dropped back as the path narrowed and they climbed into the San Juans. There were some sharp switchbacks as the peaks rose and the valleys deepened. Wallace looked over the edge at a fast-moving river and a valley thick with trees.

There was a small clearing at the top of a steep cliff ahead. Miller lifted a hand to stop them and dismounted. Wallace and Mouse did the same, then crouched as they moved forward and laid down at the edge of the cliff.

There was a Ute camp below. Flames rose from a few small campfires. They were too far away to hear any chatter, but the Utes were moving around, preparing the evening meal. Wallace counted around twenty-five warriors. He scanned the camp, they had guards posted at the perimeter.

Miller stood and showed himself about the edge of the cliff. A single warrior moved to the middle of the camp, feathers blowing in his hair. The others fell back. The warrior in the middle raised his arm. That, Wallace knew, must be Severo.

THIRTEEN
MEETING SEVERO

The three of them descended slowly down some more switchbacks and reached the edge of the Ute camp. Wallace saw about as many warriors as he'd seen from up above—around twenty-five. Only a few carried rifles—old rifles—but most had only bows and arrows. Severo barked an order, and they all stood aside to let the visitors pass through.

Severo stood alone in the center of the encampment. Miller moved forward and stopped in front of the warrior. Both raised their arms. They said something Wallace couldn't understand. Severo moved to raise the flap on his tipi. Miller stepped forward, with Wallace and Mouse moving to follow.

Severo raised his finger and shook it at Wallace and Mouse. Clearly, he didn't want them in this pow-wow. Miller pointed at them, made a motion at himself, and said something to Severo. There was a long stare-down while two warriors took away their horses.

Wallace shifted his feet uncomfortably, looking from one to the other.

Miller repeated his gesture and locked eyes with Severo, who stepped aside after a few seconds and let all three enter. Miller carried with him the blanket containing the rifle and whiskey he'd had on his horse on the way out to the camp. Wallace was aware of a trickle of sweat down his back as he stepped inside. Miller was pushing this to the limits.

There was a small fire in the center of the tipi, with wisps of smoke rising and escaping out the top. Severo sat on one side of the fire, with Miller facing him on the other. Wallace and Mouse sat on either side of Miller and slightly back of him. Wallace saw a long, straight clay pipe to one side. Peace pipe, he thought. He figured that to be a good sign.

There was a foul smell inside the tipi, only partly helped by the smoke from the fire. Wallace saw a mixture of herbs, maybe mixed with weeds and mud and partly burned, in the pipe's bowl. That had to be the source of the smell, he thought.

Severo said nothing but stared at Miller and waited. Miller leaned over and flipped up the corner of the blanket, showing Severo the Winchester 73 and a bottle of whiskey. He pushed the rifle toward Severo.

The warrior's expression didn't change, though Wallace was sure he had seen the gifts. He made no move to take the rifle. Good thing this guy doesn't know how to play poker, Wallace thought. His face doesn't show a thing.

Miller pushed the rifle a little closer and pointed again. "Gift," he said. "Gift for Severo."

Severo glanced at the gifts this time but made no move to take them. "What you want from Severo?" he asked.

Wallace glanced sideways. Miller was struggling a little, Wallace thought. Miller pointed again. "Gift to help stop the iron horse. White man taking Ute land, pushing iron horse into Ute hunting ground. Gift help Severo stop White man."

Severo's eyes looked like a couple of black marbles to Wallace. There was no expression there at all. "Want Ute to make war on White man," Severo said. "Too many White mans. More come. Many Ute warriors die. No. No good."

Miller leaned back and stared at Severo, then tried again. He pointed at Wallace. "White chief," he said. "Bring warriors to help Severo. Severo win."

Severo shifted those black marbles in Wallace's direction. Wallace cursed Miller under his breath and leaned forward. He'd seen scalps on a pole outside of Severo's tipi. He had to talk fast, or Severo would add theirs to the collection.

"Severo and his warriors not fight alone," Wallace said. "Slow down iron horse. Attack iron horse and... cause trouble. We," he said, pointing at the three of them, "bring warriors to help Severo. We...we respect Ute land. We honor treaty after we stop iron horse."

Severo hadn't moved. He was still watching Wallace. He need something else, he thought. Appeal to him as a great warrior.

"Ute Chief Ouray very weak," Wallace said. He knew he was on slippery ground now, but he thought he saw a flicker in Severo's eyes. Ouray was the current Ute chief who had made treaties with the White man. Severo had rebelled against Ouray. The warriors outside had joined him.

"Severo brave warrior," Wallace continued. "Fight against White man. Bad White men not respect Ute land. We stop iron horse, make new treaty, honor Ute land."

Severo shifted his gaze back to Miller. "Him speak truth?" Miller nodded. "White chief speak truth," Miller said. "We bring warriors, attack iron horse with Ute. Ute make trouble for iron horse. Take back Ute land. Severo—great warrior." He finished by pushing the Winchester a little closer.

Severo flicked a glance at Mouse. His lips curled in a sneer, but he returned his gaze to Miller. "Good," he said. "Severo and warriors attack iron horse. Chief"—now he pointed at Wallace—"bring White warriors, pony soldiers, help Severo stop iron horse."

Now Severo picked up the Winchester, peered down the barrel, and worked the lever. He took the whiskey and placed it behind him. He waved the rifle in the air. "Bring Ute warriors more!" he demanded.

Miller nodded. "More thundersticks," he agreed. He pointed at Mouse. "Him bring more thundersticks to Severo."

Severo stared for a long time at Mouse, then shrugged and nodded at Miller. "More thundersticks. All Ute need thundersticks. Bullets!" he added.

"More thundersticks, bullets," Miller repeated.

Severo reached out to the peace pipe, then pulled a burning twig from the fire and set off a glow in the herbs in the pipe's bowl. The foul smell Wallace had noticed before was twice as bad now.

Severo took a deep puff from the pipe and passed it to Miller, who did the same. He passed the pipe to Wallace, who took it and glanced sideways at Mouse. He hoped the kid could smoke it without gagging.

Five minutes later, they emerged from the tipi. Mouse looked about as green as the mountain grass in the encampment, but the kid had managed not to heave his breakfast in the tipi.

Wallace stepped out and looked around. Their horses were gone. A warrior waved them toward a tipi and motioned at some meat cooking over an open fire. They would have to stay the night. Hopefully, they could leave tomorrow. He didn't want to think what would happen if he failed to deliver what Miller promised, and Severo came looking for him. He would have to deliver some men to attack the railroad if he wanted to keep his scalp.

Miller moved to follow the warrior toward his tipi when a powerful hand on his shoulder held him back. He turned to see Severo, whiskey bottle in hand.

Severo stared at Miller, unblinking. "You bring thundersticks."

Miller nodded and pointed at Mouse. Severo scowled and shook his head.

"No him," he said, scowling at Mouse. "You bring." Then he disappeared back into his tipi, whiskey in hand.

There I was, huddled over a table and a map with engineers again, and things didn't look a lot better than they had the first time. Talk around the camp had it that a renegade Ute warrior named Severo had been on the prowl north of here. I had told Cleo Ward I needed to talk to the engineers and Jonesy about where we needed to be on guard, where we might be attacked.

Now that we were in the middle of the meeting, I had trouble deciding what to do first. That's it, I thought to myself, I can only deal with first things first.

"One at a time," I told them. "Where's the first place we're laying rails that the Utes might get to us? Easier than they could the rest of the time, I mean. We'll go through 'em one at a time."

That produced a lot of hemming and hawing. I stood back and let 'em talk among themselves. Jonesy produced a pencil and started writing numbers on the map and drawing circles around the numbers. I looked over his shoulder. He stopped after he'd written the number five and circled it. I was feelin' sorry I'd asked.

Jonesy finished drawing and stepped back to let me have a good look. There were five places on there: I read the names. In order, going down the trail to Silverton, we had Great Trough Creek, Elk Park, Needleton Cut, Hermosa Cliffs, and Animas Gorge. That was too many to deal with.

I looked around the circle of engineers. "Mostly,

we'll talk today about the first two," I told them. "Tell me first about the Great Trough Creek. Then Elk Park. We'll have to leave the rest of it until we get past those two. The engineering has to be your problem. Just fill me in a little on that and then tell me what the danger of Ute attack or highwaymen might be."

Everybody looked at Jonesy to speak for the rest of 'em. He stepped up to the map at pointed at the spot marked number one. "Great Trough Creek," he said, "we've already got a good start on that one, and the creek ain't but about a hundred feet wide. Mostly an engineering and building problem. Gotta lay trestles and solid support in that creek. We'll be through there in another week."

I knew I couldn't help much with that, but these guys were already at work on it, and we would soon be past the creek. I didn't bother looking at the map—it couldn't tell me anything Jonesy hadn't already said. I tapped the map with one finger while I stared out at where they were laying the ties.

"Okay," I said, "Tell me about Elk Park."

Jonesy spoke for everybody again. He didn't bother pointing at the map this time. "This is where we're gonna need your help the most," he said. "Maybe more help than anything else between here and Silverton. We've got to go through some steep passes in and out, blast it out in places to make a way through on the way out. We've got some steep canyon walls on both sides and some thick forests down there in the canyon. The Utes can come down from the passes, hide in the forest, launch attacks on us…"

I grabbed a pencil and tapped the map. I'm bettin'

my forehead was all scrunched up while I did that. My mama used to tell me not to scrunch up like that, said I would get lines on my forehead. Lines or no lines, I was scrunched.

"Holt and me will have to scout," I announced. "We'll find the spots where they could form up and we'll have to be there first, on the high ground." I stared at the line on the map where the rail would go. I needed to ride up and see how thick those stands of trees were.

"We'll have to set up some log barricades along the way, make ourselves a place to hunker down behind, and fire back if we need to. We might have to clear some trees next to the tracks along the way so they can't come on us outta those trees." I glanced at Jonesy. "I know, that'll slow us down. We'll just have to think of a way to get the time back later."

Everybody was nodding their head. "Good plan, boss," Jonesy said.

I waved my hand to end the meeting. It was all I could deal with for now. "We'll talk about those other places after these first two," I said.

They all filed out of the tent. I took one last look at the map. I didn't even want to think about Needleton Cut, Hermosa Cliffs, or Animas Gorge for now. We would have to worry about those later. I would have to talk to Ward about this. It seemed to me I was better suited to handle the first job he gave me.

I figured I could protect the line from robbers and Ute attacks, but he needed a railroadman again to run this. Like Deacon, except honest this time.

———

Joanna stopped and read the sign—*Pete's Trading Post* —this was the place she'd been looking for. She had the uncomfortable feeling somebody had been following her, but she saw nothing when she stopped and looked behind her.

A grizzled man with a huge, shaggy red beard looked up from behind the counter when she walked in. He adjusted his spectacles on the end of his nose and stared at her with curiosity.

"Afternoon, miss." He readjusted his spectacles and came out from behind the counter. "Haven't I seen you down at the bakery?"

Joanna grinned. The best way to get known around this town, it seemed, was to work at Ma's Bakery. "You did," she agreed, "but I came to ask about mining, and Ma tells me you know more about it than anybody else in town."

"Pete," he said, holding out his hand. "Tell Ma thanks, and I'll be down there for another pie soon. What kin I do fer ya?"

Joanna had decided in advance just how to ask her question. She didn't need the whole town of Durango thinking she had found gold.

"This has to do with my grandfather, Ezekiel Dunne," she explained. "He was a fur trapper and miner in this area about fifty years ago. There was a story that went around the family about how he and his partner found some black pebbles on a mesa top near here and took them to Los Angeles."

Pete's eyes opened wide and his jaw dropped.

"And," he filled in, "his partner was Barnabus Smith, is that right?"

Joanna nodded but hurried to finish her story. She was a little shocked that Pete had already known where she was going with this. Time to head him off. "It was," she admitted, "but this isn't about that old story of Barnabus Smith and the black pebbles. I know how many people have gone looking for that mesa and never found it."

"That's right." Pete nodded his head up and down so hard his spectacles nearly fell off. "Can't tell you how many people have wasted their time looking for it."

"I know," Joanna said. "I'm just mainly interested in what I can find out about my grandfather. Could he have gone mining around here? Maybe panning in the Animas River? I've always been interested in my family's history."

"Sure, could have," Pete said, tugging at his red beard. "There's been a lot of gold found out there in the river and the mountain streams feeding that river. A lot of it's already been mined, but folks bring in gold and silver flakes and pebbles all the time. What was your grandpa's name again?"

"Ezekiel Dunne."

Pete stopped and stared at the floor, then shook his head. "No, sorry, never heard of him, but that's been a long time ago. Don't know if he ever put down some roots in these parts or not."

"Okay, thanks." Joanna asked her last question as if she'd just thought of it on her way out the door. "How would gold nuggets turn black, anyway? Could that have even happened?"

"Could have," Pete said, retreating behind the counter. "Doubt if he'd have found some up on a mesa, though, less'n he carried 'em up there hisself. Gold can turn black if it's mixed with somethin' else, maybe iron would be the likeliest thing. Some kind of other metal in there with the gold. Iron will turn black. Happens faster if it's mixed with water. You can separate it out when you process the gold. Got some iron up in the hills, too. Reddish-brown looking, sometimes you can see it in the mud."

Joanna nodded like she had already lost interest in what he was saying. "Thank you," she said on her way out the door. "If you hear anything about my grandfather, come and see me at the bakery."

Stopping outside the trading post, she stopped to think about what she had just learned. Lat could be right! If Barnabus and Ezekiel had panned in the Animas River and done it in an area heavy with iron, somebody else might have done that, too. Somebody who found black pebbles and, unlike her uncle, took the pebbles with them. Somebody who maybe needed to lighten their packs up on that mesa, running from the Utes...

Joanna crossed the street to go into the general store. She might as well have a gold pan to take with her when she went out to visit the rail camp.

Miller hung around the post office across the street while the girl was in Pete's Trading Post. He'd followed her around for a few days and he'd just about lost interest. Mostly, she just worked at the bakery and went back to her room at the boarding house.

She came out of the trading post and stood on the boardwalk for a minute. She crossed the street and went into the general store. Miller yawned, pulled his watch from his pocket, and checked the time. Might as well stay for a minute to see what she buys in the store, he thought. Then he needed to find Mouse and plan how to rob this general store tonight for guns and ammo.

Miller scowled when he remembered Severo's demand. Miller had to come in person with the guns and ammo, that's what Severo had said. Fine, he would come with the first delivery. Just enough guns to get the Utes started. Then Mouse would have to earn his keep and deliver the rest. Miller had other things to do.

Ten minutes later, the girl came out of the general store and Miller's eyes widened. She was carrying a gold mining pan. He had a feeling his hunch about this girl was going to pay off soon. He turned and walked back to The Rusty Bucket.

FOURTEEN
STORE ROBBERY

The line was getting farther and farther out of town, but they could make it out and back in a few hours in the handcart. I made it a point to go back into Durango once or twice a week. I told myself it was because I needed to check in with Cleo Ward, bein' that I was new to the job and all. He always grinned like he knew better when I said that.

I rolled into town about three o'clock in the afternoon, just a few days after I'd had the talk with Jonesy and the boys about Elk Park. I was a little worried about moving the rails into that valley. We had only a day left to get past Great Trough Creek, so that was good news. I told Ward about it when I dropped in on him.

Ward leaned back, put his feet on the table, and told Matthew to take a break. He lit a cigar and squinted at me. "Elk Park's the next dangerous stretch, right?"

I nodded. "I can take Holt and maybe one or two

others with me to watch the passes, but there's a thick cover of trees in that meadow. Those Utes have a lot of hidin' spots in there if Severo wants 'em. I need a couple guys to help guard the workers while they're measuring and layin' the track."

Ward nodded right away. "We'll do it," he promised. "I've already hired me a guard to ride with the supplies on the handcart when we send out the small shipments. Too easy for somebody to hold that up and take our stuff if they want to. I'll get another two for you, at least until you're past Elk Park."

He blew a cloud of smoke in my direction and stared at me. "What else you got? You look kinda worried."

I told him what I'd been thinkin' about. "You need a railroad man to run this thing," I said. "I know about security and guarding against attack and such, but I don't know anything about the rest. Jonesy tells me stuff, and I tell him to do it. Buck tells me what's goin' on with the boys laying track, and I tell him to keep doing it. I ain't sure what you're payin' me for."

Ward snorted and squinted at me. "I'm paying you to do what you're doing. The rails are going down, the boys are safe and doin' their jobs. I've been out a few times and that's what I see. That's what I need you to do. Let Jonesy and Buck do their jobs."

I stared down at the table. "I'm not a railroad man," I muttered.

Ward swung his feet down. "This bothers you," he sighed. "Tell you what I'll do. If I can keep it the way it is until we're past Elk Park, I'll put Jonesy in charge if you'll stay with it for protection and security until we're through to Silverton." He grinned. "And bust some heads like you do if you have to. Deal?"

I looked up and nodded. "Okay."

"By the way," he said, "Ma and Joanna are ready to make the run out there and sell some baked goods in a few days."

I frowned. "I don't know if it's safe for her to go out there."

"She can take the handcart," Ward said. "There'll be a couple boys pumping that cart, and I'm getting a guard on there, remember?" He grinned. "You can ride along with her if you'll feel better about it."

I shot him a quick look, but he was ignoring me.

Ward took a couple more puffs. "What're you planning after the line goes through?" he asked. "It's a big, new country out here."

I'd wrestled with that in my head a few times, but I didn't have an answer. Not a good one, anyway. "Maybe mining," I said. "Or it might be nice to get myself a spread someday."

Ward nodded. "Think about it some more," he said. "This country's growing up, and it needs some men like you to grow with it."

I agreed. Joanna had said something like that to me the last time I was in town. That reminded me, and I stood up. "I'm gonna go get a room at the boarding house and get me some dinner."

I opened the door, and I heard Ward chuckle. "Say hi to Joanna for me," he said as the door closed.

I walked on down to Ma's Bakery. I expect I was a little red in the face after what Ward had just said. Maybe it was getting a little obvious that I stopped at the bakery every time I came to town.

The bakery was closed for the day, but I tapped at the door like Ma had told me I could when I was in town. They were in there working on things for tomorrow, I knew that. The bell tinkled when Ma hustled over to open the door for me. She gave me a big hug and took me over to the table she was calling *Lat's table* now. Joanna poked her head out of the kitchen. She had flour on her face and up to her elbows.

"Coming out as soon as I wash up," she called. "I want to talk to you."

Ma fussed over me with coffee and fresh-baked bread until Joanna got there. I started to stand when she came, just like my ma taught me, but she waved that off and took a seat.

"How is the rail line going?" she asked as she reached over to take a corner of the bread slice I'd left on my plate.

I filled her in on how we were doing. "Just about across the Great Trough Creek," I told her. "We'll be up to the edge of Elk Park and starting through there in about four days."

"Okay," she said. "Ma and I have been talking. I'll bring bread and pies out to the camp in a few days, before you really get started in Elk Park. Is that okay?"

She saw I didn't look real happy and reached out to pat my arm. "Don't worry, it'll be safe," she assured me. "I think it's cute you worry about me. Don't forget, Mr. Ward has a new guard on the handcart starting tomorrow."

I wasn't too sure I enjoyed being called cute, but I buried my mug in my coffee cup. She was getting awfully good at reading my mind when I worried about her.

Joanna got up to get me a refill on the coffee, then started in on what else she wanted to do. I wasn't sure if I was going to like it, but I was pretty sure I'd wind up agreeing to it. She was a strong-minded woman. I was finding that out.

"You said you're almost to Elk Park," she reminded me as she set the coffeepot down. "That means you're very close to the Animas River right now, right?"

I looked up in some surprise. She'd never been out there, but I knew right away she'd been studying maps and had probably gotten railroad plans or maps from Ward. No use asking, she was right.

"We are gonna be right next to it, almost, coming up to Elk Park and for a long time while we're going through there," I agreed. "Why?"

"I want to come out there on the handcart with you tomorrow," she said, grinning at the look on my face. "You'll be there, and the guard will be with me coming back," she explained. She kept going before I could say anything. "I met Pete, down at Pete's Trading Post," she went on. "He explained how gold pebbles could turn black."

My head came up. She reached out to put her hand on my arm. "Don't worry, he thinks I was just asking about what my grandfather found. Anyway," she continued, "I bought a gold pan. Maybe you could take a little time when we get there and I could do a little panning? I'm curious to see if we find any black pebbles. Just tiny ones, I'm sure. Pete would look at them to see if they have any gold when I bring them back."

I looked at her and thought it over. She moved her hand to pat mine. "Please? I promise to stay close and be careful."

I kept looking at those blue eyes and my head commenced to nodding up and down like somebody was pulling it on strings. "Okay, I'll do it," I murmured. Holt and Ward were never gonna let me hear the end of this.

We agreed to meet down at the handcart, on the tracks down at the yard, by seven in the morning. I stayed for some dinner with Ma and Joanna. It wasn't until I left the bakery and started for the boarding house that the silly grin spread across my face.

Sometimes Miller liked to sit at a table by the window in his Rusty Bucket saloon. Since Miller didn't like people, he had to have a good reason to sit out there. This evening, he had a reason.

Miller thought it was a good idea if people saw him out here and could remember him being in the saloon. Just in case the marshal got any ideas about checking up on him after tonight's robbery.

Miller had just finished going over his plan to rob rifles and ammo from the general store with Mouse, the idiot who worked for him at The Rusty Bucket. He could do without Mouse easily, that's why he was using Mouse to rob the store and deliver the goods to Severo. Miller scowled for a minute when he remembered he would have to be with Mouse for the first delivery.

Miller reached for his beer and scowled again. Normally, he would have some of his best whiskey right about now, but he had to be sharp for the robbery tonight. That meant beer. He lifted the glass to his lips as he saw something through the window that got his attention.

It was that railroad security guy, Latigo Smith. The one who'd killed Deacon and spoiled Miller's great setup stealing railroad supplies and tools. Miller's eyes narrowed as he watched Smith walk into the boardinghouse. When Smith disappeared inside, Miller's gaze switched as he stared down the street.

Smith had probably been down at the bakery with that little snip, the new one in town. Miller wondered what those two were up to. Miller's scowl changed to a thin, cruel smile as he thought about the possibility of getting even with both of them at the same time.

━━━

I delayed departure the next morning when Marshal Anderson came galloping up to the train yard and waved us down as we were getting on the handcart.

"Ma told me I could find you down here, Lat," he hollered. "Can you come with me for a few minutes?"

I glanced at Joanna and helped her back down off the handcart. How, I wondered, did everybody know they could expect to find me down at Ma's Bakery? Joanna grinned at me. There it goes, I thought, that reading my mind thing again.

Marshal Anderson trotted up and tipped his hat to Joanna. "Ma'am." He looked at both of us. "I'm sorry to interrupt. Ma told me you're on your way to the camp, but the thing is, somebody robbed the general store last night. Could I get you to take a look at things before you go, Lat?"

"Sure." I was a little puzzled. What did this have to do with me, except maybe he wanted me to take a look because I was a deputy sheriff?

Anderson turned his hat over in his hands a few times. "They just stole rifles and ammunition," he explained.

My stomach turned over a couple times. That sounded like a raid or attack of some kind was going to happen. What was a more likely target than the rail-road? We would be in Elk Park in a few days. Not good, that was what my brain was saying.

Joanna moved up beside me as we trotted toward the general store. "Robbed during the night, did you say?" I asked. "Did anybody hear anything while it was going on?"

"Nobody," Anderson said. "I've told old Jenkins at the store to lock it up better, but we've never had any trouble. Somebody just shoved through the back door. Jenkins had a lock on it, but the wood was old and the frame was flimsy. Somebody forced it open with no trouble at all."

Jenkins met us at the door. "Been double-checkin', Marshal, like you told me to. Jest rifles and ammo, that's all. Don't know why they went and made such a mess." He pointed into the store. Shelves and cases had been overturned, with merchandise laying on the floor everywhere.

"Another thing," Jenkins mumbled. "They taken three brand-new Winchesters an' left the rest of 'em. Taken eight or nine old Sharps and Henrys. I had 'em on the bargain rack. They was used and kinda old." He shook his head and wandered away.

I walked through to the back of the store. They hadn't left all that much on the shelves. Jenkins was going to have a lot of work straightening this out.

Joanna trailed behind me. "Why would they do this if they only wanted the guns?" she asked.

I turned and nodded. "Either they didn't know where to look for the guns and found 'em last, after they'd left this mess, or they were just trying to confuse us. I think they were trying to confuse us. At least for a while. I guess old Jenkins knows his store so well he knew right away they only took guns and ammo."

I stooped beside an overturned shelf and peered underneath it. After a moment, I reached and pulled a small, ragged piece of plaid blue cloth from under the shelf. Anderson kneeled beside me to look at it.

"Whatcha got?" he asked.

I handed him the cloth. "Could have come from somebody's shirt," I answered.

I walked out the back door and found several sets of bootprints. I kneeled to get a closer look. Anderson moved out to join me. "What do you make of it?" he asked.

I rose and moved down the slope in the back of the store. "I think two men," I said. I followed the prints a little farther down the slope and through some trees. They ended at a stream flowing through a gully at the bottom.

"Two men came and went this way," I muttered. "Used the stream to cover their tracks. I guess the two of 'em could carry the rifles and ammo without a horse if they brought a knapsack or a couple bags."

"You worried they want to use the guns against the railroad?" Anderson asked.

I nodded and slapped my hand against my thigh in frustration, staring down the stream. "Yep, that's it. I don't know why they want old guns. Unless they gave 'em to the Utes. Maybe somebody doesn't want the Utes to have the best guns. Gave 'em the old ones."

I turned and looked at Anderson. "I need to get out to the camp," I told him. "I'll find a way to let you know if I think of anything else."

"Thanks." Anderson stood back and followed Joanna and me up the slope and through the store. Five minutes later, the two guys who ran the handcart had it rolling toward the rail camp.

Miller stumped around in an old, uncomfortable pair of boots inside The Rusty Bucket. Miller lived in a back room next to the room he used as an office. His best pair of boots was soaked from wading in both directions through the stream. Mouse had stashed the rifles and ammo in the woods behind The Rusty

Bucket, if he had followed Miller's orders after the robbery.

Miller put some water on to boil for coffee and moved to the front window of The Rusty Bucket, careful to stay out of sight, a little distance back from the window. The general store they had robbed was just across the street and down two shops. Miller had cursed all the way down the stream until they waded out and up to a wagon he had left at the side of the trail. They had taken the wagon back and unloaded the goods in the dark. He felt sure their tracks were covered.

The water boiled, and Miller went to pour himself a cup of coffee. He spilled some on his hand and produced a fresh round of cursing, more heartfelt than what he'd been doing last night. He moved back to his spot near the window. The marshal was there, along with Smith from the railroad, and...was that the girl from the bakery?

Jenkins, the old fool who ran the general store, met all three at the door. They disappeared inside. Miller finished his coffee and decided to wear his good boots, even though they were wet. When he came back into the saloon and looked out the window, Smith and the bakery girl were walking away, arm in arm.

Miller froze and watched, not sure if he should risk following. Curiosity won out. He slipped out the back and trailed them from a distance. They went to the rail yard and climbed up on the handcart. Miller stared, unbelieving, as they rode out of town on the handcart.

He walked back to The Rusty Bucket and slipped back in the way he had come out. Miller walked into the saloon and reached for the coffeepot, then changed his mind. He broke out a bottle of whiskey. He had to celebrate. If he could catch the girl out on that hand-cart, he knew exactly what he wanted to do. He took the whiskey and walked back to his office. He didn't want to be out here in the saloon when people started showing up for work. He had some planning to do.

FIFTEEN
BLACK PEBBLES

J oanna and I stood at the back of the handcart and held on to the handles as the cart rumbled out of Durango and picked up speed. We had two guys operating the pump handles, and I agreed to apply the brakes where we needed it.

"On the downhill," they warned me. "We can't be pickin' up too much speed on some of them hills."

We picked up speed as we moved out of town, mountain peaks around us, along with rugged cliffs and valleys. The rails took some sharp turns on those narrow rails as we moved on toward the camp. Joanna grabbed hold of me on some of the sudden turns. That was my favorite part.

We settled in on a long, slow climb and Joanna opened up the subject that had been troubling me all morning. "Do you think somebody stole those rifles to arm the Utes for an attack? They could have taken some newer models instead of those old Henrys."

I nodded slowly. "I think the crew is safe until Elk

Park," I told her. "They get a lot more cover and good ground after we enter Elk Park. They say this warrior Severo might be on the prowl. He doesn't seem to be happy about the peace made by Chief Ouray. We don't need outlaws giving 'em guns to come after us. They won't be happy with the rails coming into their land."

Bert Anderson stepped into The Rusty Bucket Saloon, feeling most of the eyes in the room shifting in his direction. He'd only been a marshal for less than a year, but he'd found that when people spent a lot of time staring at your badge, they might just be guilty of something. He always got that feeling in The Rusty Bucket. When he looked at people, he felt their eyes shifting away.

Anderson pulled the piece of plaid blue cloth given to him by Lat Smith out of his pocket and took another look at it. He was pretty sure it came from somebody's shirt, like Lat had said. He wanted to have a good look at that cloth before he started looking around this saloon. He might just be able to match this piece of cloth to the owner of the shirt.

Anderson saw Miller, owner of The Rusty Bucket, staring at him. Anderson shoved the cloth back into his pocket, cursing himself mentally for having let Miller see the cloth. Miller saw way too much, and he always seemed one jump ahead of Anderson.

Ignoring Miller, Anderson stepped into the middle of the saloon. He circled the tables, feeling the eyes drop away from his badge while the drinkers and card players studied the floor. He turned back to the bar in time to see a flash of blue disappearing into the back while Miller stepped up to the bar.

Anderson moved toward the back room where he'd seen that blue flash disappear. Miller stepped from behind the bar. "Help you, Marshal?"

The tone was friendly, but the eyes were not. Anderson stared at the bar owner, noticing a little sheen of sweat on Miller's forehead. Was it hot in here, or was Miller nervous? Anderson couldn't remember Miller looking anything but completely relaxed and in charge of things.

Anderson locked eyes with him. "Well, Miller," he said softly. "You might know that the general store across the street was robbed last night. I thought that whoever robbed that store just might try to get out the back of your place or hide in the storage room if he saw me here. Do you have any reason I shouldn't look back there?"

From the corner of his eye, Anderson saw the bartender step toward the bar and reach under it.

"Hands!" Anderson shouted.

The bartender froze where he was and looked at Miller, who angled his head and nodded. The bartender stepped back and placed both hands on the bar.

Anderson locked in on Miller again. He was sure the man was sweating harder now.

Miller shrugged, stepped aside, and trailed behind Anderson as he checked the storage room, then opened the back door and stepped outside. Anderson took a long look in all directions, then stepped back inside and walked through the saloon without a word. The front door banged shut loudly behind him. Whoever owned the blue shirt had gotten away.

Miller stayed busy in the saloon for a full two hours after Marshal Anderson left, which was longer than any of his workers could remember seeing him stay. He worked the bar, joined a poker game long enough to lose five dollars, and even cleared off a couple of tables. His reason was simple: if Anderson returned, Miller wanted to be seen working in his saloon.

By mid-afternoon, he retreated to his office in the back. On his way, the bartender asked if Mouse was around to help with the early crowd. Miller silenced him with a glare and barricaded himself in the office.

He reappeared a few hours later with a sealed envelope. On the back, he had written the name of Deputy Marshal Wallace. Miller walked to the bartender and gave him the envelope.

"Wallace will be in here, jest like he is most nights," Miller growled. "Give him this." He handed the envelope over but hung on to it when the bartender tried to take it. "Nobody reads this but Wallace," he hissed.

The bartender nodded and placed the envelope on the shelf under the bar.

At dusk, Miller slipped out the back, pausing on the stoop to look in all directions. He carried a bag in one hand and a lantern in the other. They were going to have to travel at night to leave Durango. With a little luck, he could be back before anybody noticed he was missing tomorrow. The saloon didn't open until noon.

Mouse was another story. Mouse would never be back in Durango. The fool had worn a shirt all morning after tearing it in the general store last night. Anderson had a pretty good idea, Miller was sure, that Mouse was the one wearing the blue plaid shirt. That made him too big a risk. There were things Miller still needed him to do, but after that, Mouse was a dead man.

Miller walked swiftly down the trail that carried him to the woods behind the saloon. If Mouse had followed his instructions, he had waited about two hours, then gone to the livery to get both their horses and saddled them up. Then he would have loaded the rifles and ammo on the horses, where he would wait now for Miller.

There was enough moonlight to avoid lighting the lantern. Miller walked straight into the woods until he heard a low whistle. He stayed where he was until Mouse emerged from the underbrush and led him to the horses. He glanced at them critically. At least, Miller admitted grudgingly, the man had done what he was told about the horses and the rifles.

Miller circled the horses, staring critically. Each of their horses carried two of the rifles. The packhorse carried the other rifles and a crate of ammo. Mouse had probably stolen the packhorse. Miller didn't care. The livery stable owner was too scared of Miller to say anything about it.

Mouse glanced at him nervously. "What'd the marshal want?" he squeaked.

Miller shrugged. "Jest checkin' into the robbery, that's all. We'll git outta town for a while and let it settle down." That reminded him as he looked at Mouse again. He'd changed out of the blue shirt. A day too late, Miller snarled to himself.

They waited until darkness had closed in. Miller counted on following the railroad tracks after they'd left town. Once safely out of town, they could wait for daylight to go to his cabin on the Animas River. He didn't want anybody else to know about the cabin, but this couldn't be helped. It was another reason Mouse had to be six feet under after this was done.

They led the horses to the main street on the edge of town and mounted up, proceeding by the light of a half-moon. As they left town, a pack of dogs heard them and set off a racket, running at the horses and baying. Miller cursed, but he had prepared. He reached into his jacket pocket and tossed jerky at the dogs. When the dogs stopped to eat the jerky, he spurred his horse and rode away, followed by Mouse.

Slowing just a short way out of town, Miller lit the lantern, and they followed beside the rail tracks, moving slowly in the dark, but proceeding steadily away from town. By the time the first rays of dawn broke the darkness an hour and a half later, the two robbers were at the top of the first steep climb on the rail line.

Miller reined in and waited. Mouse, scared by the gruff silence and glares from his boss, simply pulled up and waited, asking no questions.

When a figure emerged and walked his horse over to them, Mouse was surprised. It was Deputy Marshal

Wallace. Mouse had seen Wallace come and go from Miller's back office at The Rusty Bucket, but this seemed like a strange place to meet. Mouse had the good sense to hold his tongue once again.

Mouse rode off a short distance, then realized one voice was getting louder as the other two men talked. Miller was shouting, but Wallace was quiet when he answered. He didn't back down. Mouse had seen nothing like this before. Miller backed off, much to Mouse's surprise. He could see how red Miller's face was, but the man had physically backed away. Wallace was shaking his head no, and he hadn't moved.

Mouse ducked a little when he realized both men had their gunhands near the holster. A long moment passed before Miller waved his hand angrily in the air and remounted. He rode past Mouse without a word. Mouse followed.

—————

Wallace stayed where he was, watching them ride away. Wallace had ridden the outlaw trail for a long time, with extended time spent operating out of Brown's Hole and Robber's Roost. Stealing horses paid pretty good, but not like that railroad deal with Miller and Deacon. Now that was gone.

Wallace had never hurt a woman, and he never planned to do that, ever. Miller had changed his plan a little and agreed to Wallace's deal when they'd argued about that. So far, he'd agreed, anyway. If Miller went back on his word…well, it might be time to have it out with Miller. Or maybe Latigo Smith or someone like him would take Miller out, and Wallace wouldn't have to. Wallace had killed several men. Mostly, they had worn badges. He grinned to himself. He was the one with the badge, lately. That would change. He watched Miller top the rise and ride away. He would wait and see, then he would deal with Miller if he had to.

The handcart rumbled in and rolled to a stop. I helped Joanna down. From the corner of my eye, I could see some guys lay down ties and move toward us. Sometimes I brought mail, but this wasn't one of those times. I shook my head at Buck and he barked at them —they went back to laying ties.

Buck walked over and shocked me. He took off his hat and nodded at Joanna. "Ma'am, welcome," he said, nice as you please. I'd had no idea he had manners like that.

"Great job, Buck," I said. "I've been talking to Mr. Ward about gettin' you more money. Keep it up." He beamed, looked at Joanna, and nodded.

I looked down the slope at the Animas River, which was rushing around a bend only thirty yards away. "We're going down to the river for a while, Buck," I said. "You need anything from me right now?"

He shook his head and went back to the crews. Joanna reached into her bag and pulled out a mining pan. I lifted my Winchester from the handcart, and we made our way down to the river.

We reached the river, and I rolled up my britches to wade out with the mining pan. "Have you ever done this before?" she asked. "That river is moving awfully fast."

"Sure," I said, wading out. "Just watch this." I waded out, stepped around a big rock, and set my foot down on a flat rock just below the surface of the water where the algae could get a foothold. My foot shot out from under me and I folded up like a tent, landing on my backside.

"Are you okay?" she called.

I picked myself up, but I left my dignity down there in the river. "I'm okay," I said, massaging my rump.

I could hear her trying not to laugh, but first, she sputtered a couple times, then just leaned over, put her head in her hands, and downright howled with laughter.

I flopped down beside her on the bank. "I'm plumb...I'm glad I brighten your day so much," I grumped.

"I'm sorry, I shouldn't have laughed, but the way you got up, it was, well, it was kinda cute."

I was trying to decide if I liked being cute when I felt her hand on my cheek. She turned my head, leaned in, and planted a kiss right on my lips.

I felt that tingle all the way to my toes. I can't recall being that surprised. Well, maybe when I was a kid and walked behind my horse without patting his rump first, then got kicked in the shins for my troubles. This was way better than that surprise, of course. Maybe I didn't mind being cute.

Joanna jumped up, rolled up her pants, and grabbed the mining pan. "My turn," she announced. She waded out, being way more careful than me, then bent and dipped up some gravel and water. She swirled it around in the pan until most of the water was gone, then waded out with what she had left.

We both took a look in the sunlight. Not much except gravel, I thought, but there in the corner, was that a black speck? Joanna saw it too. She reached into her pocket and pulled out a little pouch. She put the black pebble in the pouch.

We took turns working at it for a couple hours. When I heard Cookie ring the triangle for lunch, I told her I needed to get back to the camp. I stood and reached a hand down to help her up.

"We have enough," she said. "They're all tiny, so I know they're not worth much, but I can have Pete at the trading post process it and tell me if there's any gold in there. It might solve the mystery of old Barnabus and Ezekiel's treasure, anyway. They weren't right here, of course, but maybe somewhere on the Animas River."

We walked up to the lunch line. Holt had come in. He was grinning at me like a chimpanzee, but I ignored him. I would hear about it later.

After everyone had eaten, I walked Joanna back to the handcart. She gave me a hug and hopped up. The two fellas running the handcart didn't have me to work the brake anymore, but they seemed to have it handled. Joanna waved as the handcart rumbled around a corner.

Miller led the way toward the river, glancing back at Wallace a time or two and letting his anger ease up. What kind of fool was Wallace, too softheaded to do anything to the woman? Nobody was going to know about what they were doing here, anyway.

The cabin came into view, nestled away among some cedar trees, a stone's throw from the Animas River. Nobody else knew about this. He planned to keep it that way once Mouse was gone.

Dismounting, they both tied up their horses and walked inside. Miller threw his bag on a bunk in the corner. He waved his hand at the rest of the cabin. "You sleep on the floor or outside," he rumbled. "Take yer pick." He grabbed a cane pole with a line and hook on it from its perch on the wall and stomped outside.

Grabbing a little shovel leaning against the outside wall of the cabin, Miller dug some worms, baited the hook, and walked down to the river to catch some dinner. "Git a fire going," he growled over his shoulder. "Won't take but five minutes to catch our fill of trout. Then we'll talk about getting them rifles to Severo and his braves."

Joanna carried the small pouch with ten to twelve black pebbles into Pete's Trading Post and waited while he served another customer. She browsed a few shelves and waited, reminding herself she shouldn't show much excitement, no matter what Pete said.

When it was her turn, she stepped up to the counter. Pete grinned. "Granddaughter of an old-time prospector. Forgot your name, sorry."

"Joanna." There was nobody else in the store now, so she was hoping to do this quickly. She opened the pouch and shook the dozen black pebbles onto the counter. Pete adjusted his spectacles. His eyebrows rose as he looked up at Joanna.

"I just went out to the river with a friend and thought I'd have a little fun panning in the Animas like my grandfather might have done," she murmured. "We didn't come up with much for our trouble, but I'm just curious if these pebbles might have gold in them."

Pete said nothing but turned behind him to pick up a long knife. Joanna suspected it was extremely sharp. "May I?" Pete had the knife poised over one pebble.

Joanna nodded, and Pete pressed down, splitting the pebble in two. He carried one-half over to the light spilling through his window and examined it carefully.

After a minute, Pete returned and placed the pebble on the counter. "I'd say this pebble has some gold in it. Not much, of course—it's so small. Probably not very high quality. I could get it processed for you, but there might not be enough gold in these pebbles to pay for it."

"No thanks," she said, sweeping the pebbles back into the pouch. "It was mostly just for fun, anyway. Maybe my grandfather found pebbles bigger than these somewhere." She turned away from the counter and waved over her shoulder. "I'll be back if I strike it rich." She laughed. Pete grinned and waved as she left. He'd seen dozens of people consumed by gold fever over the years he'd been here. He hoped this nice girl wouldn't be another one. Still, he thought, she had found these pebbles in the Animas River...

SIXTEEN

DELIVERING THE GOODS

They left the cabin at daybreak, loading the horses with the rifles and ammo as before. Well, Miller snickered to himself, Mouse had loaded them while Miller had some coffee. Leaving at first light was important, though. Severo and his warriors would be up at daybreak. Miller knew that. Severo would have no respect for a man who wasn't up and moving at first light.

Miller knew the journey would take about three hours. He led the way on narrow paths that climbed sharply and unexpectedly before plunging into a valley with tall pines and thick underbrush. Occasionally, the underbrush covered the trail, but Miller knew his way. The tricky part was to sell Severo on doing what Miller wanted. Miller needed the railroad to look to him for protection. Protection was what Miller would offer.

Rounding a final switchback, they saw Severo's

camp below them. The Ute warriors hadn't moved camp since Miller's earlier visit. He smelled meat from the cookfire—probably venison—and herbs as they rode in. He glanced at the pole next to Severo's tipi. The scalps were down. Miller's stomach knotted as he prepared to tell Severo he had only half the rifles promised. He needed to hold the rest until Severo could ready another attack. Miller's gut told him one attack wouldn't be enough to stop the railroad. He couldn't count on Severo attacking twice if Miller had given him everything he wanted on today's visit.

Severo emerged from his tipi as they dismounted. The morning sun sharply outlined the scars on his face. Miller stood and waited for Severo to speak. Mouse stood behind him. Miller could hear Mouse's heavy breathing and mentally cursed him for his fear. Severo stood staring at them for a long moment.

Severo then pointed at the packhorse, and two braves unloaded the guns and ammunition, then carried them to a spot just behind Severo's tipi. Severo followed the braves and motioned at Miller and Mouse to follow him.

The two braves pried the lid from the ammunition crate and left. Severo pulled the blanket off the guns and checked them one by one, sighting down the barrel and grunting from time to time. He set the Winchesters aside and picked up the first Sharps.

"Old," he grunted, staring at Miller.

"More new guns coming," Miller said hastily. He pointed at the Sharps rifles. "Good guns. More new ones coming. Soon."

Severo prowled around, inspecting the rest of the rifles and the ammo. He settled down on the ground cross-legged, a deep scowl on his face. Miller and Mouse sat as well.

"All warriors need thunderstick. White man has thunderstick, warriors have bow."

"Soon. More thundersticks for all warriors." He pointed at the rifles. "Severo and his brave warriors take these, attack White man in Great Valley." Miller wasn't sure what Severo called Elk Park, but he was sure the Ute chief had men watching the progress of the rails. He would know what Miller meant.

Severo said nothing for a full minute. Miller shifted uncomfortably on the ground but held the Ute's stare. Severo shifted his gaze to Mouse, and Miller could hear the kid gulp. Last mission, Miller told himself, this was definitely the last mission for Mouse.

Severo stood suddenly and held up two fingers. "Two suns," he said. "Two suns, attack White man in Great Valley. After that, you bring White warriors. Help Severo."

Miller and Mouse stood rooted for only a moment, then hurried around the tipi. Two braves held their horses, staring at the White men without expression. Clearly, they weren't being invited to stay this time. They mounted and rode out at a slow, steady pace, careful not to look back.

Out of sight around the switchback, Miller reined his horse around to look for any warriors following them. There was nobody on their trail. Mouse heaved a vast sigh, and for once, Miller agreed with him. That had been a touchy moment back there.

Miller turned his horse, not wanting to talk, but Mouse pushed the issue. "What now, boss? Back to the cabin? Watch the attack when they make it?"

Miller spoke over his shoulder. "Back to the cabin for you right now, but you'll be watching when they attack the rail line in Elk Valley." He glanced backward. "Don't worry, you'll be safe. You might even have some fun with it."

Miller looked forward again. "I have some business back in Durango. I've got to get there today and I'll be gone a few days. I'll meet you at the cabin three days from now." They rode the rest of the way to the cabin in silence. Mouse stood in the clearing at the front, holding the reins to his horse and the packhorse. Miller rode away without another word.

━━━

Several days had gone by and it was time to go to town again. The handcart boys had stayed at the camp overnight after yesterday's trip, along with the new guard Ward had assigned for the handcart. We started out early the next morning, headed to Durango to pick up Joanna and the delivery from Ma's Bakery.

I handled the brake again so the guard would have his hands free. The San Juan Mountains towered over us as we rumbled down the rails. Every man in that camp would have some money in his pockets and one eye on the rails, watching for the handcart to come back in.

We rolled into the station at Durango a few hours later, and I hopped down and headed for the bakery. I got delayed when Cleo Ward popped out of the rail-road office and flagged me down.

"I know today's the day for the bakery delivery." He grinned. "I'd go with you to deliver the good news, but I've got to take a train to Denver and meet with some of the railroad big dogs."

"Big dogs?"

Ward chuckled. "That's just what I call the guys that control the purse strings and make the big deci-sions. Big dogs."

"Oh." I filed that one away in my head and asked the other question. "What's the good news? Besides the fact we're bringing the goodies today."

Ward grinned again. "The baked goods are gonna be free. Half paid by the railroad as a reward for the good progress you're making. Half paid by Ma herself. You can ask her why when you get there."

"Okay." I was still just as curious, but I would find out in a few minutes. I hustled on down to the bakery, more to see Joanna than to ask Ma questions. But I could get both things done and be on my way to the camp soon with Joanna. I was hoping I could get there without chowing down on all the food myself.

The bell tinkled as I walked through the door, just like always, but was it my imagination, or were Joan-na's hugs getting a little stronger every time? I hoped I wasn't imagining. I stepped back from the hug, and the smell of the delivery was overwhelming. The pies and bread were all packaged up and ready to go, lying on a table in the dining area.

Ma came hustling out of the back, waving a towel in the air. "Got a horse and buggy all hitched up out back," she announced, "ready to get those things down to the rail yard."

I followed her out the back with the first armful of pies, stepping carefully. The boys back at the camp would string me up if I dropped the pies. Ma showed me the crate she had on the buggy and told me how to pack 'em in there to keep them as protected as possible on that bumpy handcart ride.

"Is it true?" I asked, "All these goodies are gonna be free for the boys up there at the camp? You'll be the most popular human in this town."

"True," she beamed. "Railroad is paying half, and I'm paying the other. When that railroad gets through to Silverton, it's going to double my business down here. And when any of those boys up at the camp come through town after this, they'll be coming through my door with their money."

I couldn't argue with her on that one. Ma was a great baker and a pretty sharp business lady as well, it looked like. We finished loading, and I climbed into the buggy with Joanna, waved goodbye to Ma, and made the quick trip down to the rail yard.

Joanna laid a hand on my arm to stop me before we climbed down from the buggy. "Got to tell you what Pete at the trading post told me about those black pebbles," she murmured.

I was all attention.

"Those pebbles do have a little gold in them. Not enough to be worth processing this batch. If we found more that are larger and maybe a little purer, though, that would be a different thing altogether. Maybe it's true that some trapper got several of those pebbles right in the Animas River! Maybe your uncle and my grandfather found some there, too. They could have washed down from the mountains up there and gone through soil with a lot of iron when they settled at the bottom."

We stayed on the buggy for a minute while I thought that one over. "We've got to look for more, but I don't know how, with the crew going into Elk Park and the Utes maybe havin' been armed by somebody," I muttered. I thought for a minute. "If there's better, bigger pebbles and nuggets, they're probably farther upstream in the direction we're going."

The handcart guys and Ward's security man were hopping down off the cart and moving over to help us load things. Joanna held on to my arm for a moment when I moved to get down from the buggy.

"Holt," she said. "Maybe Holt could help us. He's out scouting for food all the time, right? And he's watching for deer and elk coming to the river for a drink? We could include him in this and he could look for more of them."

"Perfect." I patted her hand and reached to help her down. "We'll talk to Holt when we get there," I murmured.

The handcart crew came swoopin' down on us, staring into the crate and just about drooling. "Easy, boys." I grinned. "Load 'er up gentle and get us there in one piece. We'll have something for you guys at the other end, I promise."

Ten minutes later, they had the crate loaded and braced on the floor of the handcart. Next thing I knew, we were rumbling out of town, heading for some hungry guys up at the camp.

━━

Miller and Mouse stood well back from the rail line, kerchiefs over the horse's noses to prevent them snorting at the sound of the handcart. They watched from the trees. When the handcart had moved past, Miller gave the signal to mount up and follow.

As they fell farther and farther behind the cart, Mouse shot puzzled glances at Miller, but he knew better than to open his mouth and question his boss. Miller waited until they were about an hour out of town before speaking.

"We don't care about stopping the cart on the way out there," he finally explained. "We're going to stop it on the way back and take the girl with us."

Mouse spent a full minute to decide whether he had the courage to ask a question. He rolled the dice and took the chance.

"How…uh, how are we gonna stop it, boss?"

Miller, feeling good because his plan seemed to be working, honored the question with an answer.

"They'll just have the girl, two handcart operators, and the guard. You an' me are gonna drag a log across the rails and hide. Deputy Marshal Wallace will hold up his badge, tell 'em a tree fell across the rails, and ask 'em to help drag it out of the way. We take 'em down while they're doing that, and then we take the girl."

Mouse's face was a study in confusion. Miller took

pity on him. "Wallace," he explained, "is with us. You and me come out, guns up, and tie them up. If they fight us, shoot 'em. Oh, and when we're done, we pretend to tie up Wallace too, so the folks in town still think he's doing his job."

Mouse absorbed the plan slowly, then shook his head in wonderment. "You're a genius, boss."

Miller grunted. Too bad, he thought, that it was an idiot telling him he was a genius. Otherwise, it might mean something.

━━━

The work crew had actually moved into Elk Park, with the rails running down toward the meadow for several hundred yards. I had the boys stop the handcart before we started down to the meadow. Mostly, I was trying to save them the work of getting it back up to the top when they started back. The other thing is, I didn't feel it was as safe for everybody down there. This way, the workers would have to come out of the meadow and up to us.

The steep cliffs rose on both sides, left and right, but I knew those Utes could climb down like mountain sheep if they wanted to. They knew these peaks better than anybody, and that was a danger. We just stopped the cart up at the top and watched those hungry rail workers charge in.

I stood at the front of the cart and waved my arms to stop 'em, which I thought was pretty brave of me. "We've got the goods, and I've got good news," I bellowed at the top of my lungs. "But you gotta line up down there and promise not to stampede us."

Buck got them lined up and even kept a couple guards posted watching for the Utes, like I'd always insisted we do. "Put your money away," I yelled. "It's free. Paid for by the railroad and Ma's Bakery. A loaf of bread and a pie for everybody. You can buy more if there's anything left over."

I had Joanna handing out the food, which made everybody mind their manners, if they had any. The guard watched like a hawk until she was done. The food was gone in fifteen minutes. Holt worked his way over to me, grinning from ear to ear.

"You're the most pop-u-lar man on this here railroad," he said, wiping the last of the pie away from his face. "Won't nobody be bellyaching if I don't get some meat for tonight."

Joanna hopped down from the cart and came over. "Did you ask him about it yet?" she asked.

I shook my head while we all moved off a little way from the others. I checked over my shoulder to make sure the guards Buck had posted were still on the job. I didn't want to spoil this party, but we'd be in poor shape if anybody attacked right now.

Finally, I relaxed and turned back around. Joanna was pulling the pouch out of her pocket with the tiny pebbles we had found. She spilled them out into her hand. Holt bent over her hand to look, then shook his head. "Little black pebbles?" he asked.

Joanna and I swapped looks. "There's a little gold in the middle of 'em," I explained.

"Huh." Holt bent down for another look. "How kin you tell?"

Joanna explained how she had taken them to the trading post. "Haven't you ever heard the stories about Barnabus Smith and the black pebbles?" she asked.

Holt gave us both a blank look. "I'm jest a country boy from Tennessee," he mumbled. "If this Barnabus guy found the pebbles out here in Colorado, I wouldn't know about it." He stopped and stared at me. "You kinfolk to his Barnabus guy?" he asked.

Joanna told him the story about my uncle and her grandfather. Holt listened, nodded, and kept looking at the black pebbles. He took off his hat, scratched his head, and whistled. "I'll be a dad-blame polecat," he announced. He looked back and forth between us. "Why'd you tell me about it?"

"If there're more pebbles in the Animas River," I said, "bigger pebbles with more gold in 'em, we need help to find them. We'll share. You're always out there, scouting and hunting along the river. Have you seen pebbles or black nuggets like these?"

Holt closed his eyes and thought it over. "Maybe..." He turned and stared down toward Elk Park. "Maybe down there, where the meadow climbs up toward the peaks. There's a waterfall or two coming off the San Juans back in there." He shook his head. "I'd have to look up in there again...but maybe."

Buck was moving toward us, and the boys were moving around again. Until now, they'd mostly been laying on their backs with their bellies in the air, but

Buck had 'em moving again. "Ready to start laying those rails, Boss?" he boomed.

"Ready," I told him. "Be there in a minute." I turned back to the others. "We'll talk more about it later," I said. I took Joanna by the elbow. "Time to get you back to town."

———

Severo pressed himself to the ground, staring through a notch in the peaks rising over Elk Park. The twelve warriors he had brought with him were to his right, arranged on the western side of the meadow. They had come in the early morning hours, planning on a surprise attack to drive the invaders out of the valley. Now, the invaders were gone.

Severo had left his warriors and worked his way to the north, trying to see where his prey had gone. He stretched out on the ground and extended the prize possession he had taken from a pony soldier several years ago. He knew that when he pulled it out and stared through the end, he had the eyes of an eagle.

He balanced the old spyglass on a boulder and stared down toward the far end of the valley, then snorted in surprise. There was something on the silver rails, but it wasn't an iron horse. This was much smaller, it was standing still. He raised his head and stared. What made that thing move? He shifted his position to see beyond whatever that was on the rails.

They were back there, moving around. All the White men were still there. Severo put his eye to the spyglass again and watched. There were guards at the entrance to the valley. He could see them. Moving the spyglass one more time, he double-checked the valley below. No one was working on the silver rails.

Severo settled down to wait. There was nothing they could do now, but when they came back to start work on the rails, he would move back and order the attack. Until then, his warriors would wait for him to come and give them the order. First, he would move them down from the peaks to take a position in the trees at the bottom of the slopes.

SEVENTEEN

TROUBLE TIMES TWO

I headed back into Elk Park with the crew after watching the handcart pull away. Joanna waved from the cart and got a few cheers of *hip-hip-hooray* from the rail workers for her trouble. I could see her laughing as the cart disappeared around a bend.

We walked down into the valley, following the rails already laid over the last several days. When we reached the end of the rails, I realized we hadn't done something I wanted to do when we first entered Elk Park. The workers were too far from cover, and the heavy trees on the slopes on three sides could shelter anything or anybody. It exposed us to attack.

I moved ahead to where Buck was picking the crews and assigning work. I tapped his shoulder.

"I need you to assign about four guys to cut down some trees and drag 'em alongside the tracks while the rest of the guys are measuring and laying the rails," I told him. "We're too out in the open, and anybody that wants to come after us has all the cover in the world."

Buck picked out four hefty guys and told 'em they could use his horse to help drag the trees over. They grabbed a pair of crosscut saws from the supplies and set off to give us a little cover. I heard footsteps coming up behind and realized Holt had followed me down into the valley. He moved alongside.

"Good idea, pard," he said, his eyes sweeping the surrounding trees, then moving up to watch the peaks. "I ain't been hearing many birds down here."

I turned and stared at him. I couldn't believe I hadn't noticed it myself. Usually there were birdcalls going on all around us. Now, not so many. I swung in a slow circle, watching and listening. Especially on the western side, I thought, it seemed a little quiet.

"Buck," I called, "set a couple more guys to help with those logs. Have two more with Winchesters watching over them while they work. They can take my horse to help them drag logs." I turned around to Holt. "You too, Holt," I said, "keep the rifle handy and move around as you see fit. Keep a sharp eye out. Something's not right."

I picked up my Winchester and field glasses. I would roam around like Holt and watch. Birds don't stop singing for no reason. We could afford to slow down the pace of the work for a couple days.

━━━

Severo stared down the slope. The iron horse workers were cutting down trees. He muttered to himself, then snapped the spyglass shut and began moving to his left. His warriors were waiting on the western peaks for his commands. He had to start them down the slope now. There was still time for an attack. He shook his head and stared down the slope again. The big one in the black hat—he was the one giving the orders and getting the white eyes ready for Severo's attack. They had to get into attack position soon.

━━━

Joanna was smiling as the handcart pulled away. The crew had appreciated her bakery run beyond what she would have imagined. Several had given her money and insisted she give it to Ma. For the first time, she turned her thoughts to the possibility of opening her own bakery in Silverton. Not right away, but when the trains were running from Durango.

The security guard was a withdrawn, severe man, and Joanna had learned not to talk to him. He was all business, but she had to admit she was glad for the extra protection. Latigo seemed very concerned about the safety of herself and the crew.

The handlers for the handcart were a different matter. She had made a couple of runs with these guys now, and they couldn't be more different from the security guard. Zach was the older man, a veteran of several years working on western railroads. Joanna knew he had chosen to settle in Durango with his family, tired of the long days away from home, laying rails.

The young man, Adam, was only twenty years old. He'd wanted to sign on to the rail crew, but he'd come a little too late for that. He had caught on with the railroad by working on the handcart and hoped to move to the rail crew at his first chance. Joanna glanced at him sideways and grinned to herself at the floppy black hat and prominent Adam's apple. She could almost spot him from across town.

Watching the snowy peaks sliding behind her in the background against a foreground vision of colorful wildflowers, it caught her completely by surprise when the boys applied the brakes. The stop came suddenly and violently. Caught unprepared, Joanna pitched forward and banged her head against the front rail of the cart, then slid to the floor.

Stunned, she tried to get to her feet but slumped sideways, back down to the floor of the cart. The world seemed to swim in and out of focus. She touched her forehead, and her hand came away bloody. The security guard kneeled over her anxiously.

"Miss Joanna," Adam said, wringing his hands as the security guard pushed him back. "We're awful sorry, ma'am," he moaned, "but there's a giant tree trunk done fell across the tracks. We had to throw on the brakes so as not to jump them rails."

Joanna grabbed the hand offered by the security guard and struggled up to one knee, her brain struggling to make sense of things. An unknown voice came from her left, adding to her confusion.

"Easy, folks," the voice said smoothly. "Just got here myself. I'm the deppity marshal in these parts." Joanna turned her head slowly, and the shine of a badge came into view. She struggled to put a name together with the voice.

"Wallace," she whispered to herself. "And I know Lat doesn't trust Wallace."

"You boys just climb down and help me pull that tree trunk off'n the rails, and you can be on yer way in no time," the voice went on. "It'll take all of us to shift it. Ma'am," he continued. "You just stay where you are. You've had a nasty bump. We'll get you into town."

Joanna heard Zach and Adam hopping down off the cart. She wanted to shake her head, but she couldn't seem to move it much. The security guard was still kneeling beside her, trying to make sense of what she was mumbling.

"Crooked deputy, I think," she said, pushing the words out with as much force as she could. "Don't trust…crooked."

The security guard let go of her arm and rose on one leg, his hand sweeping down for his gun. Two shots rang out from the shrubbery beside the rails and the guard pitched over backward, rolled heavily to his side, and dropped off the cart.

Joanna swung her head desperately toward Zach and Adam, but they were standing with their hands in the air. Deputy Marshall Wallace held a gun on them. While Joanna watched, a server she recognized from The Rusty Bucket moved behind the handcart handlers. He reversed his grip on his Colt and dropped them both with blows from the handle of the gun.

Footsteps sounded behind her, then a hand grabbed her hair and yanked her head back roughly. Someone slipped a hood over her head and tied it down around her neck. She felt a gun barrel on her back. She was too stunned by the blow to her head to offer resistance.

"Hands behind you," a voice snarled.

She knew that voice...her mind scrambled to think where she'd heard it. At the bakery, she knew that. Several faces flashed across her mind, and then she knew. It was Miller, that guy who owned the saloon. The one who'd wanted to know too much about her. It was him.

His voice was muffled, making her think he was wearing a bandanna over his face. Her instincts told her immediately not to let him know she'd identified him. Much safer for her if he thought she didn't know him. She moved her hands behind her back and let him tie her up.

She yelled with pain and surprise when those hands pulled on her hair and yanked her to her feet. A hand pushed her forward a few steps, then stopped her. The same rough hands grabbed her and lifted her from the handcart, carried her several steps, then slung her over a saddle. She felt the rope around her hands being cut, then she felt the man retying her hands to the saddle horn.

Listening was the only thing she could still do, so Joanna concentrated on what she could hear. The voice she'd identified as Miller's talked with Wallace, the outlaw deputy. They were arguing, but they were far enough away she couldn't hear the words. Now she thought she could hear someone, probably Miller, walking back in her direction.

Moments later, Miller was talking to somebody

else, probably the server from the saloon. They were closer to her now, but talking in soft tones. A horse moved away. Joanna could hear nothing from Zach and Adam. She knew they must still be unconscious. Footsteps came close to her, then she felt the motion of her horse as someone led her away. She knew she was alone with Miller. The security guard was dead, she was sure of that.

Miller was livid as he stalked away from Wallace and moved over to talk to Mouse. He'd insisted that Wallace kill the two cart handlers—they had seen Wallace's face and might make the connection with Miller. Wallace refused. Miller had considered drawing on Wallace and finishing things up right then and there, but a little voice told him not to. It was fear of Wallace. He knew that, and he hated himself for it.

Muttering under his breath, knowing Wallace was watching him, Miller stalked over to Mouse and reached into the little canvas bag he'd brought with him this morning. He reached into the bag and pulled out something wrapped in old newspapers. He handed it to Mouse, who opened it and stared inside. The package contained a stick of dynamite. Reaching into his saddlebag, Miller handed over a few matches.

Mouse's mouth dropped open, and he stared at Miller. "W-w-whaddya want me to do with this?" he stammered.

"Cause trouble up there at the railroad," Miller hissed. "By the time you git up there, Severo will probly attack the crew. I want the railroad to think it's not jest the Utes comin' after 'em. I want them to think the whole world's comin' down on them. I want them to think they need my protection bad."

Mouse looked at the dynamite, then back up a Miller. His jaw worked open and closed a couple times, but he didn't come up with a question. He just stared.

"I don't care," Miller hissed. "Just throw it—throw it wherever you want to. Blow up the supply tent if you want, or take out some crew. Just give 'em something more to worry about."

Mouse snapped his mouth shut and nodded. An idea got started somewhere in that brain. The more he thought about it, the better he liked it. That high-and-mighty Latigo Smith, the one that punched so hard, that's who he would throw this stick of dynamite at.

Mouse worked his tongue around the right side of his mouth, where there was one molar missing and another one still loose. He owed this to Latigo Smith. That's who he would throw the dynamite at. He couldn't wait.

Wallace watched as Mouse rode away first, going north. Probably going up there to make more trouble for the railroad, Wallace thought. Miller rode away next, leading the spare horse with the girl tied in the saddle. Wallace didn't like that. He might have done something about Miller taking that girl, but the security guard had been murdered. Now there was a kidnapping on top of it. And that warrior Severo expected him to bring help he wouldn't be bringin'. Time for Wallace to clear himself out of here. Swinging at the end of a rope wasn't part of his plans.

Wallace walked over to where the cart handlers were lying in the grass, tied up hand and foot. One lay still, the other was moving a little and moaning. Wallace kneeled beside them, pulled a knife from his belt, and cut the rope tying the hands of the one who was still out cold. He didn't mind robbery, but he wouldn't leave these two to be killed by predators or found by the Utes. A man deserved a fighting chance.

Wallace walked to his horse, swung aboard, and turned the animal to the west. He pulled the badge from his shirtfront and tossed it over his shoulder. He was done here. Time to go back to the outlaw trail. He could steal some horses and add to the money he'd stashed away while he made another plan. Maybe California, he thought. Or maybe he would stay on the outlaw trail for a while. Brown's Hole and Robber's Roost were both places he knew well. That was a good place for a man to make another plan.

―――

The men had been felling trees and dragging the logs back to place them near the rails for two hours now. I had lent them my horse and had Holt patrolling on foot so they could use his horse as well.

I lent a hand with the saw where I saw men getting tired, and my words to them were always the same. "Cut 'em down at the edge of the tree line, and drag them back as fast as you can. Don't worry about lining them up right now. The more you cut down, the less cover anybody has to attack."

I passed the saw back to one of the crew and went to check in with Holt. "Whaddya think?" I murmured.

"I think it's way too quiet out there, Lat," he said, never taking his eyes off the trees. "I think they're comin' from the slopes on the west, and they're coming soon. How we doin' on laying down some cover?"

I turned and looked at the logs on the western side of the rails. I counted five long logs lying there, with another one on the way. They had just felled one more at the edge of the trees and were hitching that one up.

"I think we've got enough to give cover to everybody," I muttered. "I'll have 'em drag in that one last log, then they can cut it in two and lay it an angle at both ends. That'll give us a flank." I walked off, then turned back. "Come on in and help set up the defenses," I said. "If they're out there and they see me call 'em in, they'll come in a hurry."

I walked out to the crew, who had just reached the defense line with their log. "Lay that one next to the others," I said. "Then I'm gonna have you and the rail crew act like you're breaking for chow. You're gonna carry all the ammo to the logs instead, then all the guns and lay them behind the logs. Be ready for anything."

The boys pulling in the last log reached the defenses. "Cut it in half," I said. "Lay half at an angle at each end. It'll give us a flank. Keep one eye peeled and be ready for anything. If nobody's out there, just consider I gave you boys an extra break."

Mouse hunched down at the edge of the valley, watching things develop. He knew Severo planned an attack today, and he had driven his horse hard for the last hour to get here, thinking he might be too late. Instead, he saw Smith's crew preparing and laying out defenses. Mouse stared at the western slopes, cursing under his breath. He'd hoped to do nothing but clean up after the Ute attack and even his score with Latigo Smith today. He wanted the Utes to do the dirty work.

He crawled closer, keeping under cover of the mountain cedar trees to the east of the rails and defenses. At least he had that going for him. They all had their backs to him, and he could get close. Another twenty yards, and he could throw the dynamite and just about reach the angled log at the south end. Smith seemed to have taken up position there.

I took the southern flank and told Holt to take the north. We both had pistols, plus Winchesters, so we had more firepower than the rest of the crew. I would keep an eye out behind us too, we didn't need a sneak attack taking us out from the east.

The attack came as the boys hustled in and passed out the rifles, and it took me by surprise because it was a silent attack. A dozen or more arrows came from the woods. One man, not quite down behind the logs, cried out, grabbed his leg, and fell. Two others dragged him to cover. Another man grabbed his shoulder but made it to cover and picked up his rifle.

The boys answered with a barrage of fire, but I could see only one brave fall, sliding out from behind a cedar tree. I was pretty sure Holt had scored that one. I couldn't see a target, which meant the crew couldn't, either.

"Save your ammunition," I yelled. "Don't fire unless you're sure you can see something. They're just trying to draw fire."

A few more arrows searched the surrounding air, but the boys were down behind the logs and nobody had to tell 'em to keep their fool heads down. An occasional shot rang out. I saw one brave lurch out from behind a tree, grabbing at his leg. I dropped him with a shot to the chest.

It got quiet for several minutes. "When they come," I said, "let 'em get closer. Hold your fire until you've got somebody square in your sights, then cut loose."

Another two minutes went by, then the valley erupted in gunfire. They came from behind the trees, unbelievably close, screaming that wavering war cry. I saw one of our men go down.

They held fire for a moment longer, then we all cut loose. The ragged line of Utes went down here and there, and several of them weren't getting up. The rest darted back into the trees. I saw one brave dragging a wounded man and shot him as he reached the trees. The rest melted away.

I rested my Winchester against the log and told

everybody to hold their positions. Then I glanced behind me and felt the shock run clear through me.

Mouse was standing in the trees behind me. I could see a stick and a spark of fire and he was getting ready to throw something. It could only be dynamite, and he was close enough to get it here.

"Down on the other side of the log!" I screamed as I palmed my Colt and fired. The bullet drilled him dead center in his chest, but his arm was already coming forward. He fell as the dynamite left his hand. I turned and dove for cover on the other side of the log.

There was a tremendous explosion, a lot of dirt flying, then blackness.

EIGHTEEN
THE SIDE ROOM

I could hear people talking to me, but I couldn't understand why they were so far away. I opened my eyes and stared through the dust at Holt. He was only a foot or two away, and from the ways those jaws were goin' up and down, I figured he was talking to me, only he wasn't making much noise. That wasn't like the Holt I knew at all.

I pushed myself off the ground and sat up. One hand stayed on the ground to stop the wobbling. I looked past Holt and saw most of the crew gathered around him, and some of them were talking at me too. There was a lot of dust swirling. I remembered the Ute attack, and I remembered shooting Mouse just before the explosion.

Somebody brought some water, and I gulped that down but stayed there, just roosting on the ground for a while longer. The ringing in my head let up some, and now I could hear things a little better. Holt put out his hand and pulled me to my feet. We took a tour around the camp.

Holt steered me away from the rails and the western slopes where the Utes had mounted the attack. He pointed at a crumpled figure on the ground, lying at the foot of some cedar trees. We got closer, and I knew who this was and why he'd brought me over here first.

"Ya done put paid to this one," Holt said, leaning in so I could hear. "I seen him back in Leadville, I think. Nothin' but trouble back in Leadville, too. What was his name? Rat? Whiskers? Some kind of crazy name."

"Mouse," I said, staring down at him. He had two bullet holes near his heart. "He had him a stick of dynamite he was fixing to throw at me. Got him just in time, I guess."

"Reckon you did," Holt agreed. "Got him plumb center, I'd say." He waved at two railway workers and told them to bury the body. Then he led me toward the woods on the western slope. The Ute attack had come from here.

"Utes are gone," he explained. "I taken a look-see while you was off in dreamland. They done pulled their freight."

There wasn't much left to see—the Utes had taken their dead and wounded, like always. Holt kept an eye peeled up the slope and kept his Winchester handy while I looked around the base of the slope. There were some broken branches and a few patches of blood on some tree trunks. I followed a path for a short distance, trailing the footprints and splotches of blood in the dust. I left off trailing and came back to Holt. There wasn't much to see, and I hadn't expected much. He watched me and waited.

"How many do you reckon we got?" I asked.

Holt shrugged, then leaned over and spat. "I reckon mebbe seven or eight kilt and two or three more got some lead in 'em," he answered. "Close to half the war party, I'm guessin'. They won't wanna tangle with us no more, or they won't have a war party left," he observed.

I nodded, and we moved back down toward the work crew. They were still manning the post beside the logs we'd laid out for defense. As we got closer, I saw them turn and stare back down the rails. As I watched, I saw the handcart rolling down into the valley. Zach and Adam hopped down off the cart, waving at me and yelling.

Holt's mouth dropped open, and he trotted toward Zach and Adam, then he stopped to stare back at me. I ran to catch up. When I got close enough to hear them, my stomach turned over, and I felt the blood rushing to my face.

Severo stopped at the top of the ridge after his braves had moved over it and started down the other side. He stared down into the valley, feeling the wind blow hard against his face. He had lost too many braves today. They would go back to camp and find the medicine man to help his wounded braves. There would be no more fighting for now.

Severo watched as the chief in the black hat walked into the cedar trees below, bending to read the signs in the brush. Severo shook his head and waited until the chief in the black hat walked away. That one, he thought, had powerful medicine. Maybe they would meet again someday.

He turned, crested the slope and moved down the other side until he reached his braves. He leaped astride his pony and led them away. For now, they would have to let the iron horse pass through.

I knew what they would tell me, even before I got close enough to hear.

"They taken her!" Zach was waving his arms and charging toward me. Adam was a step behind.

It was no use asking what had happened. The handcart should have been back in Durango by now. They skidded to a stop in front of me.

"They taken Miss Joanna," Adam yelled. "They taken our pistols and hit us on the noggin. They kilt the security guard!"

"Easy," I said. I felt the blood rushing up into my face. I was going after Joanna, and somebody was going to pay for this, but I needed all the facts I could get. I motioned at a log. "Sit down and tell me what happened. Zach, you do the talking. Adam, you fill in whatever else you can think of."

They sat, Zach took a long breath, then told me how they'd been stopped by a log across the trail. "That deppity sheriff, Wallace, he stepped out an' told us to help 'em move the log. There was a couple voices talkin' back there in the bushes, then somebody tied us up an' conked us over the head. Somebody had already untied me when we come to. Ever'body was gone. Hoss tracks goin' off in two different directions. Two hosses went east, one went west."

I listened, feeling my gun hand clench and unclench while they talked. I figured one of the three was Mouse. That left two alive, and one of those was Wallace. The third one, I knew, must be Miller.

"Okay," I said, "the three of us are goin' back to where they dropped that log across the tracks." I glanced around behind me. "Somebody get these boys a couple of guns." I swung around and looked at Holt and Buck. "Keep laying those rails," I said. "I'll be back in a couple days."

Cookie tossed some water and a little food on the handcart and we jumped aboard. They led my horse up on the cart and I grabbed his reins to keep him still during the ride. Holt reached up to pass me a box of ammo. I knew the horse could help pull us when we needed it. "You sure you don't want me to come?" Holt asked.

"No," I growled. "Miller can't hide from me and he's gonna answer for this. When I find him, I'll find Joanna. I just hope I'm not too late."

———

Her captor said nothing. Joanna listened for any clue about where they were going, but she heard no streams or falls—no moving water at all. She put her mind to work—her captor, Miller, was in front of her, leading the way. She could hear the clip-clop of his horse's hooves and the occasional squeak of saddle leather.

Her hands were bound to the saddle horn, but she could feel the ruffle of lace around her sleeves, and it gave her an idea. She would have to gamble that Miller wasn't looking back to check on her. With the hood over her head, she could only hope he wasn't. She closed her fingers over the lace on her left sleeve and ripped it free. For several minutes, she held the torn lace in her hand. When she felt the horse pulled to the left by the rope attached to Miller's horse, she dropped the lace to mark her trail.

They moved on with no comment from Miller, so Joanna busied herself, tearing the ruffle loose on her right sleeve. Minutes later, when she felt another jog in the trail, she dropped the second marker. Again, there was no comment from Miller. It was only a small victory, but maybe Lat would see the markers on the trail. She had no doubt he would be coming.

Keeping track of the time was difficult. She tried estimating the minutes and counting them off in her head, but they might have been on this trail anywhere between a half hour and two hours. She felt brush and branches rubbing against her legs on both sides. That meant the trail was narrowing.

Now she could hear a rushing stream. The sound grew louder as minutes passed. Joanna thought it was unlikely to be a major river, but the noise kept growing as they got closer. This, she thought, could be the Animas River. In another minute, they stopped moving. Miller still said nothing. She heard a door open and slam shut. Finally, she heard footsteps approaching, and Miller yanked the hood off her head.

Joanna blinked against the late afternoon sun. There was a weather-beaten old cabin standing at the edge of the river, which she could now see was about twenty feet wide. It rushed past and bent around a curve downstream. As happy as she was to have the blindfold removed, Joanna knew this was a bad sign. Miller didn't care that she could identify him. That didn't bode well for her future.

He cut the ropes binding her to the saddle horn, then reached up and yanked her from the saddle. She stumbled as she hit the ground. Miller cursed, grasped her upper arm, and pulled her into the cabin. He shoved her into a wooden chair and used more rope to tie her firmly in the chair. He carried her bag and a blanket into a side room, came out, picked up a rifle, and left the cabin without a word.

Joanna guessed he was gone about an hour. She heard a single gunshot, then nothing until Miller returned. He entered the cabin carrying what looked like two backstraps of venison, which he carried into the kitchen. He banged around in the kitchen for a while, then left again, returning shortly with firewood. Joanna could hear him building a fire in the iron stove she could see in the corner of the kitchen.

When Miller came out, he laid a rifle and a shotgun against a corner in the cabin, then used the knife at his belt to cut the ropes he had tied around her. He pulled her into the kitchen. "Cook the meat," he snarled, then pulled up the same chair to watch. Joanna took a quick look at what he had laid out on a table in the kitchen. There was a semi-rusty iron skillet, two backstraps of venison, some salt, and some oil. She poured a little of the oil in the skillet and set it on the stove to heat.

Choosing her words carefully, Joanna looked at Miller. "The backstraps won't fit in the skillet," she explained. "I'll need to cut them in half to cook them."

Miller's eyes strayed toward a drawer underneath the old sink in the kitchen, then he quickly changed his mind. Cursing under his breath, he pulled the knife from his belt and moved toward the backstraps. Joanna forced herself to remain calm and stepped away from the meat. Miller cut both chunks of meat in half and returned to his chair.

Joanna stepped in to pick up the salt, dusted the first piece of meat lightly and set it into the iron skillet. Miller seemed bored now, but his eyes never left her. She turned the meat occasionally, wondering all the time what was in that bottom drawer Miller had looked at before changing his mind.

There was a sudden whinny from one of the horses outside. Miller leaped to his feet. He turned to leave, then turned back to look at Joanna. "Don't move," he growled. Then his boots thundered across the old cabin floor and she heard the door slam behind him.

Joanna knew this might be her only chance. She whirled and yanked open the drawer Miller had been looking at. There was another old skillet, a mallet of some kind, and a cutting knife! The knife was old but looked sturdy, with a blade about eight to ten inches long.

Joanna grabbed the knife, pushed the drawer shut,

and rushed into the side room where Miller had taken her bag and a blanket. She pulled the bag open, dropped the knife in it, and hurried out. She'd had a vague impression that the side room was a place where he'd kept captives before. There was a sturdy door with a lock on it and a side window covered by an iron grill, with two bars running horizontally and another two vertically.

She rushed back into the kitchen and was back in place, turning the meat, when Miller came back into the cabin. He stood in the doorway and looked at her suspiciously.

"This first one will be done in about ten minutes," she informed him. "Do you want me to cook them all now?"

Thrown off by the question, Miller stared at her for a moment, then nodded. "Cook 'em all now," he huffed. He returned to his seat in the wooden chair, saying nothing about the noise outside.

The rest of the afternoon passed without him tying her up again, though his eyes never left her. She finished cooking the venison. Miller ate hungrily, but Joanna managed to choke down only a few bites. She tried asking Miller a question.

"What do you want with me?" she asked, looking him directly in the eyes.

Miller avoided the eye contact. He flushed angrily for a moment, then shrugged. "Yer boyfriend seems pretty nosy," he mumbled. "I aim to make him a lot less curious about business that ain't got nuthin' to do with him."

He said nothing else that day. As the sun began to

set and darkness crept in, Miller lit an oil lamp, but he was clearly tired of watching her. He fished around on his belt and came up with a key. He pointed to the side room, and Joanna walked in. The door slammed shut behind her and she heard the key turning in the lock.

With the remaining light she had, Joanna examined the room. The walls all seemed solid, and she had no hope of forcing the door open. She looked for any loose boards in the floor but found none. That just left the iron grill in the window.

The cement around the bars was ancient and cracked. She scratched at the base of one bar and found that a little cement came away when she did. Joanna walked to the corner of the room and lay down on the blanket. She did not know if she could remove the grill by prying away the cement with the knife. If she could, it would have to be done by morning. She was pretty sure she could fit through the window if the grill was gone.

She could do nothing more until Miller was asleep. There would be enough moonlight to try what she had in mind. She hoped Miller snored. That would tell her when she could get to work with the knife.

⌐—⌐

The trip back in the handcart took longer than I thought. It didn't help that I was helpless to do much of anything until we got to that fallen log. I offered to help pump the cart, but those two had themselves a rhythm and teamwork going. All I could do was ride along, hold the reins to my horse, and apply the brakes once in a while. I wondered where Miller might have taken Joanna. He'd taken her to get at me—I was sure of that.

The log was a lot farther down the track than I had thought. Maybe Miller had planned that, too. It was a long ride to get back to where they had taken her, which gave him more time to get away. We'd left the camp while we still had some good afternoon sun, but it was getting on toward late afternoon before we crested a rise and the boys put on the brakes.

I hopped down as soon as we stopped and led my horse off the cart. We hitched up my horse to the log, and we all grabbed and lifted while I urged my horse to move out. It took several tries, but we inched that big log off the rails. I was fretting at the time delay and pouring sweat all at the same time, but we finally got it shifted out of the way.

I waved at the boys and moved to mount up, but I could see they weren't moving.

"We kin hep," Zach offered. "We're mighty fond of Miss Joanna and we'd like to hep you track down whoever done this."

I only hesitated for a second before I shook my head. "I'm mighty appreciative of that, boys," I said, "but I think this here's a one-man job, and I need you to get to town. I need you to tell Marshall Anderson he needs to git out here. I need you to tell him that his deppity is no dang good. I expect he might know that already, but I need you to tell him. I'll find Joanna, I promise you."

"What're you gonna do with him that took her?" Zach asked.

I swung aboard my horse. "Bury him, I expect," I said.

They hopped back on the handcart and took it on down the line. I leaned over and followed the tracks. He hadn't bothered to cover them. I guess he wanted to get to a hideout first and worry about the rest of it later. Miller had to know what happened to a man that messed with a good woman out here. A rope was the kindest end he would see if we caught him.

The trail was a pretty straight one, and I started to hope I could catch up before sundown. There was a rumble overhead, and I glanced up, worried. Rain would wash out the tracks. I urged my horse forward until I came to a fork in the trail.

I stopped and stared as a drizzle started to fall. The tracks were a little fainter out here and the trail a little narrower, but the fork to my left seemed the most promising. I slowed my horse and followed along, then stopped when I saw something fluttering in the brush on my left.

I dismounted and reached into the brush to pull out a piece of cloth. I stared at it. It looked like a piece of lace. My hopes rose. Joanna's shirt that morning had lace at the end of her sleeves. She had found a way to mark the trail!

I pushed on, but the rain was washing out tracks and the heavy clouds overhead were taking away my light as the evening fell. I pushed on to another fork in the road and dismounted again. I could not tell this time which way they had taken.

I cast back and forth on foot, looking for any signs I could find. Ten feet down the trail on my right, I found another piece of lace cloth. I ran back to my horse and mounted again to follow this fork, but another ten minutes on the trail and I knew I had to stop for the night. The light wasn't good enough to go on. If I took a wrong turn, no telling how long it would take in the morning to pick up the trail again.

Angry and frustrated at the delay, I picketed my horse and gave him some water from my canteen, then rolled up in my slicker under a big tree branch just off the trail. I would have to wait until I had better light in the morning.

NINETEEN
RIVER RENDEZVOUS

I t had seemed like an eternity last night before Miller had finally gone to sleep. She'd heard a few bottles clinking out there and she figured that's what had finally put him under. She didn't have to wonder for long if he snored—it was thunderous.

The knife she had slipped into her bag yesterday had worked. She'd been able to scrape away at the old and cracked cement around the iron bars and pry it out in small chunks, but the process had been painfully slow. Luckily, the cement was ancient and had some cracks in it already. A hammer would have helped, but she didn't have one. Anyway, she was worried about the noise. She'd been able to pound a little with the handle of the knife, and luckily, the bars weren't sunk too deep into the cement.

Hours had passed, though, and her hands were blistering badly. Perspiration ran down the back of her shirt despite the chilly night air. Now, it looked like a bit of gray light was showing in the east.

Joanna paused and rested for just a few minutes. The snoring from the other room was still loud and regular, which gave her a little comfort. The bars on the bottom and sides were free—she just had to pry the two at the top loose. She had tried shoving at the grate, but it still held.

Joanna picked up the knife by the handle and pounded gently at the cement around the top bars. She was rewarded by seeing deeper cracks in the pale light. She redoubled her efforts, prying the cement loose, ignoring the pain from her hands. Her bag was on the floor beside her. She was ready to toss it out the window and follow it outside as soon this grill came loose.

The snoring stopped, and she froze in place. What would she do if he came in? She had pushed all the pried-loose cement out the window so it wouldn't be immediately obvious what she'd been doing all night. She decided that if he came in, she would hide the knife in her clothes and hope he didn't notice what she'd been doing to free herself from this room.

The snoring resumed. She breathed a sigh of relief and redoubled her efforts. If Miller was coming out of that deep sleep, she needed to be out of here. The snoring sounded a little more fitful now. When the grill gave way, it came out so suddenly that she lost balance, tripped over her bag, and landed on the floor. The grill had gone out the window and landed next to the cabin wall.

Excitement flooded over her as she bent, grabbed her bag, and tossed it out the window. She was prepared to follow when she realized the snoring had stopped again. Joanna pulled herself up to the window ledge, trying to pull herself through, when the door swung open and Miller let out a roar.

Joanna didn't have time to get through the window. She dropped to the floor and whirled, grabbing the knife off the ledge and hiding it behind her.

Miller closed the gap between them in two leaps, cursing as he grabbed her throat with both hands. He shoved her back against the wall, his breath reeking of whiskey and cigarettes. Joanna felt those hands cutting off her air. She had just one chance.

Swinging the knife out from behind her and around, she plunged it deep into Miller's thigh. He roared again, but this time, it was a roar of pain. He staggered back, grabbing the knife handle and screaming in pain as he pulled it out. He was bent double, with his hands on his knees. The knife clattered to the floor.

Joanna took one step and launched a kick, connecting with her right boot flush to Miller's jaw. He fell to his back, moaning and trying to rise. She sprung to the window, jumped, and pulled herself through, landing on her bag just outside. She grabbed the bag and ran for the cover of the trees, thankful the light was enough to guide her.

Treading her way through the trees, she worked her way toward the river, hoping she could use it to cover her tracks. She risked a glance over her shoulder just once. Miller was framed in the window, cursing loudly and trying to force his way through. Just as she'd thought, he was too bulky to fit. Joanna turned back toward the river, took three steps, then waded in.

She half-swam, half-waded to the other side, where she instinctively bent and picked up a rock. It wasn't much of a weapon, but at least it was something. She stayed in the water for several yards before wading out on the opposite bank.

Reaching a clump of cedar trees surrounded by some thick brush, she moved deeper into the brush and crouched down. She wasn't under any illusions. When Miller came, he would bring his rifle, or the shotgun, or both.

⸺

Back at the cabin, Miller clawed his way back out of the window and collapsed to the floor, cursing in volleys at the pain in his leg. He grabbed the bloody knife and cut a strip from the blanket on the floor, then knotted the cloth around his leg. He limped into the kitchen and downed the rest of his open whiskey bottle.

Miller limped to the corner of the cabin and picked up both his shotgun and his Winchester rifle. He wasn't a very good shot with the Winchester, but he might need it. He preferred to use the double-barreled shotgun or his pistols up close. He checked both for ammunition, making sure he only needed to cock and fire the shotgun.

All thoughts of using the girl to force Latigo Smith out of town were gone. He would kill them both—first the girl, then Smith.

Negotiating his way down the cabin steps, Miller sucked in his breath at the pain as he came off the bottom step. He limped around to the window on the side and, even in the dim light, had no trouble finding her bootprints. They led him down to the river.

Miller struggled down to the tree line, leaned against a tree trunk, and stared at the boot prints disappearing into the Animas River. He scanned the river downstream, a cruel smile coming to his lips. He would find her. She was on foot and had no weapons now. He pushed away from the tree trunk and worked his way slowly along the river bank.

Joanna saw him coming slowly down the river bank. She hadn't been able to wade far downstream before she knew she had to come out and get under cover, so the next several seconds were crucial. Miller was carrying both the rifle and the shotgun. She pulled back farther into the bushes, looking around in desperation.

There wasn't anything else she could use as a weapon. She had only the rock she had picked up on her way out of the river. His fingers curled around it as she glanced down. It was, she thought absently, a black rock.

I was already up and waiting impatiently for some light to get me going. I had an old biscuit and a piece of jerky inside my belly. Those would have to pass for breakfast. Now I needed enough light to see the trail.

The big question was how much of a trail last night's rain had left.

Finally, I couldn't wait any longer. I saddled my horse but led him forward on foot, reasoning that Miller must have stayed on this path as long as there wasn't any place to turn off. That seemed to be the case for about ten minutes, as I saw no trails leading away unless you wanted to get scratched up pretty bad in the underbrush on your way. That would have left some broken twigs and branches behind anyway, and I saw none.

My luck ran out just as I was getting some decent morning light filtering through the cedars. The trail at that point showed a small turnout going off to my right. I moved down the turnout for ten or fifteen yards, looking for any tracks left there. I didn't see tracks, so I returned to the main trail, following a few dim hoof prints. I could only hope Miller and Joanna had left these on their way through.

I mounted up for the first time, and I pushed forward at a little quicker pace, worried again about what Miller might do to Joanna. I rounded a bend and pulled up when the sound of rushing water came to me faintly from somewhere up ahead. I urged my horse forward again, figuring it made sense that Miller might have a hideout somewhere on the river, what with the freshwater he could find there.

When I heard an angry shout, I knew I was close. I pushed forward as fast as I could along that narrow, twisting trail. The path opened and widened a little as I heard another bellow out there in front of me. In another couple of minutes, I burst out from the trail and saw a beat-up old cabin with two horses out front.

I left my horse at the edge of the clearing, pulled my Winchester from the saddle, and moved forward on foot. I couldn't see anyone as I approached the door of the cabin.

⸻

Miller limped along the river bank, cursing as he looked for signs of bootprints coming out of the river on either side. He knew the girl had gone into the river, he had seen the tracks going in. The river was too deep to wade very far. Besides, she would be out in the open if she had stayed in the river.

Miller had gone only fifteen yards when he saw the telltale prints going up the opposite bank. He shouted in triumph and looked into the trees on the other side. He could see the girl moving! He chuckled in anticipation. This, he thought, was going to be fun. He would make her pay for stabbing him in the leg.

⸻

Joanna saw him coming. She stayed down in the brush, hoping against hope he wouldn't see the trail of bootprints where she had emerged from the river. When he stopped and looked at the bank below her, a cruel smile spreading across his face, she knew he'd found her spot. She rose and turned to run. At least, she thought, she had a chance to outrun him, with that bad leg of his. It was a slim chance, she knew, but if she could find enough cover in the trees...

She heard a shout behind her and glanced over her shoulder. He had spotted her. She turned to run when she heard another voice. It was a voice she knew well.

———

I approached the front door slowly, hearing nothing inside. I laid the Winchester down as I eased up the steps. It would be pistols or hand-to-hand if I found Miller inside. Slipping up toward the front door, I stopped when I caught movement from the corner of my eye.

I turned and saw Miller limping along the river bank! I dashed down the front steps and closed the distance between us. I heard him shout and raise what looked like a double-barreled shotgun.

"Miller!" I screamed. He turned, lifting the shotgun. I palmed and fired my Colt as he touched off both barrels. My left arm and shoulder stung from the pellets, but he'd fired a little too soon. My shot turned him and he staggered back, struggling to straighten up as he racked the shotgun.

I fired again, taking him dead center in the chest. He collapsed backward into the river. He splashed around a time or two, then lay still in the water as the river carried him downstream.

"Joanna!" I was desperate as I ran toward the river.

I heard a splash to my right just as I heard my name. Joanna was half-wading, half-swimming toward me. I waded in to pull her up when we met in the river. She fell into me and we collapsed together on the bank.

"I'm okay," she said. "You got here just in time."

Half an hour later, we were still sitting together, holding on to each other and listening to the river rush past us. I'd been lucky—most of that shotgun blast had gone past me. I had three or four pellets in me, which she'd pulled out gently and then washed me off in the river.

After a while, Joanna looked down, opened her hand, and held out what she'd been carrying in her hand.

"What's that?" I asked, lifting it from her hand.

She said nothing, just waited while I got a good look at it. I hefted it and stared. "It's a...black rock." My jaw dropped wide open.

"I found it on the river bank," she explained. She reached up, put both hands behind my head, and pulled me down for a kiss.

"I think we should go looking for some more," she told me.

TWENTY
SILVERTON

SIX WEEKS LATER

$\mathbf{M}$a's Bakery was quiet after the morning rush. I'd never been there mid-morning before, and I was enjoying sitting there with Joanna. Ma told us both to keep a seat while she cleaned up in the back.

"Three thousand dollars," I mumbled, holding Joanna's hand and staring out the window. "Old Barnabus was onto something, after all. I wonder if those rocks we found were about where your grandfather saw some black pebbles?"

Pete, down at Pete's Trading Post, had handled things for us, keeping it all quiet in exchange for us telling him where we found the rocks. It seemed like a fair enough deal to me. We could live our lives without folks following us around and setting off a gold rush. If Pete found some gold up there, good for him. We'd found all we could up there on the Animas

River, where Miller had taken Joanna prisoner. Spending the rest of my life looking for more...well, that's what old Barnabus had done, and it hadn't turned out that great for him.

We had agreed to give five hundred dollars of the money to Holt. He'd had my back all the way, and the railroad was almost through to Silverton now. He'd earned it. We planned to tell him about it when he stopped by here later.

"I know what I'm going to do with mine," Joanna announced, interrupting my thoughts. Ma took a seat at the table. It looked to me like she already knew about this.

"I'm going to open a bakery over in Silverton," Joanna said. "When the railroad gets there, that town will boom. Lots of miners and railroad workers. I'll be ready with the bakery." She glanced across the table at Ma. "Ma is going to close up here for a week and come over to help get me started," she said.

"Least I could do." Ma grinned. "Them railroad workers of your'n, Lat, they'll make me a fortune, buying all the bread and cookies and pies I can send out on that handcart. I don't mind taking a break and helping Joanna get started."

That left me wondering what I would do with my share. I had a good idea Holt would want me to throw in with him opening a saloon in Silverton or some-where, but I didn't want to spend my life running a saloon.

The door opened and closed, and Marshal Anderson walked over to sit down at our table. I'd been in town a few times over the last six weeks, but I always seemed to miss out on meeting up with the marshal.

He sat down and stared at what was left of the cinnamon roll on my plate. His Adam's apple bobbed up and down a few times. Joanna popped up and came back with some coffee and a roll for him. Anderson's eyes lit up when he saw the roll.

"Severo done gone to ground, that's what I'm hearin'," he told me between bites. "Nobody's seen hide nor hair of him lately."

"He might not have enough warriors to carry on the fight now," I said. "Holt figgered he lost half his war party when he attacked us in Elk Park. In any case, the railroad's gonna get through to Silverton now before he can do much else."

I picked up a spoon and stirred my coffee for a minute. "What about Wallace?" I asked. "You ever hear anything about him?"

Anderson finished off his roll and shook his head. "Nope. He just disappeared from around these parts. He can't operate as a deppity no more in Colorado, though. Word is out on him here. Somebody told me the other day he might have gone to the outlaw trail. Maybe over at Brown's Hole, up Utah way."

I thought that one over and shrugged. Didn't sound like we'd be crossing paths again, and that was all right with me.

"You ever think about becomin' a deppity again yourself?" Anderson blurted. "Railroad's gonna be through to Silverton before you know it, and I could use a good man. You've got experience as a lawman and all."

I looked over at Joanna. I could see she was interested in my answer. I shook my head. "Don't think so," I said. "I'm not sure what I want to do after the rail goes through to Silverton, but I don't think I'll pick up the badge again. Not sure what I'll do," I admitted.

Anderson dropped a quarter on the table and stood. "That's what I thought you'd say," he told me. "You change your mind, you know where to find me."

Things got quiet for a while, then the door popped open and Holt breezed in and took a seat where Anderson had just been. "Hey, Pard," he boomed. He took off his hat. "Ma'am," he said to Joanna, looking back and forth between us with a twinkle in his eye.

"Well, if it ain't my best customer," Ma said from the doorway. She disappeared into the kitchen to make Holt's breakfast. I wondered if she had enough groceries back there.

Joanna took my hand and leaned in. "We have some good news for you, Holt," she started. "You remember about my grandfather and Barnabus Smith and the black pebbles?"

Holt chuckled. "Shore, I remember. You two have looked for more of them pebbles, I know. I've done some lookin' myself."

"We found some," Joanna blurted. "Big pebbles. Rocks, in fact."

Holt's jaw dropped, and it didn't come back up in the five minutes it took Joanna to explain about that day back on the Animas River. She told him how Pete, down at the Trading Post, had processed the rocks and paid us.

"Well...I'll be..." Holt's voice trailed off.

"Five hunnerd is yours," I blurted. I waited for his reaction.

It didn't seem like Holt could focus on me for a minute there. His mouth opened and shut a couple times, but he didn't manage to say anything. Not like Holt at all.

"You've been my partner, had my back for a while now," I said. "None of this would've happened without you. Joanna and I talked about it. We want you to have five hunnerd. Open that saloon you've always flapped your jaws about. I'll be there and have the first whiskey. I expect it to be on the house, of course," I added.

Holt didn't seem to be able to say much at all. I knew he'd get over that in no time.

He left us about a half hour later with a full belly and a head full of dreams about his own saloon. It sounded like he was thinking about opening one in Silverton.

After Holt was gone and Ma was in the kitchen, Joanna hung a Closed sign on the door and walked back to the table. She sat on my lap and gave me a little kiss.

"What about you?" she asked. "What are you going to do?"

That was a hard question. I fiddled with a spoon on the table and thought. Silverton seemed like the place to be, but what would I do there?

After some silence, Joanna leaned back to get a good look at me. "Can I make a suggestion?" she asked.

"I'd be plumb grateful," I said.

"Silverton's going to be a boom town, with the railroad and mining. I know you don't want to live in the town or run a shop, but there's some wonderful land near there. It's high up, but the land can support hay and cattle."

"A ranch?" I asked. "You're saying I should start a ranch?"

"It's an idea," she agreed. "You could run a few head of cattle and raise hay. There's talk of more railroad lines going in. What if you let them put in a stop at the edge of your land? They'd need wood and water for the trains. Any hay or cattle you sell, you could load them on right there with no trouble and make a good profit."

A little smile crossed my face. "That last part was the best part." I chuckled. "The profit part, I mean. Let me think on it."

"You do that, sweetie." She got up and went to the kitchen to help Ma with some dishes.

That Joanna, she was a persuasive woman. I put my hands behind my head and stared at the wall as a grin started to spread across my face.

"Silverton," I mumbled to myself, "that has a nice sound to it."

HISTORICAL FOOTNOTE
THE LEGEND OF PEGLEG SMITH

The character of Barnabus Smith is roughly based on the story of "Pegleg" Smith, a mountain man, trapper, trader, and horse rustler in the Old West. Pegleg lost one leg after an Apache attack in 1827 and was subsequently fitted with a prosthetic—known as a wooden leg in those days, of course.

Many versions exist of the story about Pegleg Smith and the Black Pebbles, but here is one of them:

Around 1837, Pegleg and another man were bringing furs to the town of Los Angeles, probably traveling along the Colorado River in Nevada. A dust storm drove them to get their bearing at the top of the tallest of three mesas they could see after the storm had settled. There, Pegleg found black pebbles with a metal substance at the core. Thinking it to be copper, they took it to Los Angeles, where they were told it was gold.

Pegleg celebrated the news by getting into a brawl at a saloon. He was kicked out of town. On his way out of California, Pegleg and unknown accomplices stole around three to four hundred horses. Pegleg went to New Mexico, planning to sell them there. He later wound up running a trading post on the Oregon Trail in Oregon, where he specialized in selling horses, of course.

Sometime around 1853, more than fifteen years later, Pegleg organized a group to search for that mesa where he had found the black pebbles. They couldn't find it, and Pegleg deserted the group. His later years were spent hanging out at saloons and telling his stories to whoever would buy him a beer.

No doubt Pegleg's stories grew as time went by. Many searched for the mesa. A few claimed to have found it, but for the most part, the story of Pegleg and the black pebbles is one of the mysteries of the Old West.

A LOOK AT BOOK TWO

LATIGO'S CHANCE: BOOMTOWN GOLD

In the untamed heart of the American West, Latigo Smith is in for the fight of his life.

After overseeing the construction of a narrow-gauge railroad, Latigo has decided to settle in the rugged town of Silverton, Colorado. Partnering with a close friend, he opens a bustling saloon and supports his beloved Joanna in establishing a charming bakery. But his dream of owning a ranch is met with challenges.

When Latigo encounters a desperate man being forced off his land by a notorious outlaw named Penfield, he purchases the land and aids the man's family in their escape, putting himself in Penfield's crosshairs. Meanwhile, miners are being systematically robbed of their gold, and determined to help, Latigo leads a daring operation to reclaim the stolen ore.

As Penfield's ambitions grow, and he sets his sights on controlling Silverton, the townsfolk look to Latigo as their only hope. But in a lawless town, he must summon all his courage and wit to protect his new home and end a dangerous outlaw's reign of terror.

AVAILABLE OCTOBER 2024

ABOUT THE AUTHOR

Patrick Lindsay came to Texas by way of Missouri, Canada, and California and has been proud to call the Lone Star State his home for more than forty years now. He retired in 2017 from "another life" as a CPA, whereafter he turned his hand to writing.

He has read just about everything by Louis L'Amour and first decided to give Western writing a try on his initial day of retirement. He has been writing ever since and loves the idea that so many people get enjoyment from his work.

Patrick and his wife Michelle live on a cattle ranch near Fort Worth along with cows, horses, chickens, and a very spoiled Great Pyrenees dog. He is an avid fan of the St. Louis Cardinals in baseball and the Kansas City Chiefs in football.